Hurry Please I Want to Know

HURRY PLEASE I WANT TO KNOW

stories

Paul Griner

Sarabande Books

LOUISVILLE, KENTUCKY

Managing Editor
Sarabande Books, Inc.
2234 Dundee Road, Suite 200
Louisville, KY 40205

Library of Congress Cataloging-in-Publication Data

Griner, Paul.
    [Short stories. Selections]
Hurry Please, I Want to Know : stories / by Paul Griner.—First Edition.
        pages cm
    ISBN 978-1-936747-95-5 (pbk. : acid-free paper)
    I. Title.
    PS3557.R5314A6 2015
    813'.54—dc23

                                        2014004573

Cover by Kristen Radtke.

Interior layout and composition by Kirkby Gann Tittle.

Manufactured in Canada.

This book is printed on acid-free paper.

Sarabande Books is a nonprofit literary organization.

amazon.com.

The Kentucky Arts Council, the state arts agency, supports Sarabande Books with state tax dollars and federal funding from the National Endowment for the Arts.

For the Mahans, past and present

What shall we do tomorrow?
What shall we ever do?
The hot water at ten.
And if it rains, a closed car at four.
And we shall play a game of chess,
Pressing lidless eyes and waiting for a knock upon the door.
Hurry up please its time

—T.S. Eliot

CONTENTS

Animati • *3*

Newbie Was Here • *7*

The Only Appearance of Rice • *27*

The Wind, It Blows Forever • *31*

Hotei • *41*

Why I Like the Blues • *49*

A Sharp Winter, an Obese Smile • *59*

On Board the *SS Irresponsible* • *63*

Immanent in the Last Sheaf • *85*

Find Your Real Job and Do It • *89*

The Caricaturist's Daughter • *97*

Betrayal • *115*

The Builder's Errors • *119*

Mum on the Rocks • *125*

Trapped in the Temple of Athena • *133*

Lands and Times • *143*

Separate Love • *151*

Balloon Rides Ten Dollars • *167*

Open Season • *173*

Rock, Paper, Scissors • *191*

Home for the Holidays • *205*

Three Hundred Words of Grief • *209*

Acknowledgments • *225*

The Author • *227*

Animati

We were going to surprise him from the closet. He was going to be surprised when we jumped out, we didn't doubt that. He was just a temporary extension of us, and besides, we'd told him we couldn't come. Our shoulders bumped in the dark, and we had to be careful not to hit the hangers. At first we had giggled, knowing he wouldn't be there for a while, but the longer we stayed in and the more likely it was that he'd soon arrive, the more we quieted. At last it was only our breathing. Our breathing and the scent of deodorant. Of sweat. Of minty breath and whiskey breath. There were so many of us, stretching away behind me, rank after rank. I began to wonder: How many were there?

I was glad I was in front, that I'd get the chance to be first. I had so much I wanted to tell him. What do you intend? he was going to say. To surprise you, I'd tell him, clutching him to my chest so he'd feel my heart. All those years it had been beating, and now I wanted him to touch it. Palm under my blouse, warm flesh to cooling flesh, wrinkled fingers sinking into my creped skin. He was so old! But I was old too. Our hearts would beat the same. Then it would be his turn to be in front, to decide who we were waiting for next. I was yet to go forward but I could feel myself slipping back into the embrace of those fanning out behind me. Did the back ranks even know who we were waiting for, or were they turned in another direction, awaiting something else?

Hurry please. Please, please hurry. I want to know.

Newbie Was Here

When we came into the storage yard, Sergeant Bitterroot told everyone to hit the shade.

Sweetpea—the only nickname I'd caught—said, Seriously, Sarge?

It's how we roll, Sergeant Bitterroot said.

A group huzzah, followed by a few guys calling out, You're the bomb!

I'm down with that, Sarge, I thought, though of course as a replacement I hadn't earned the right to say so yet. Still, I dropped my pack with the others and was about to express my appreciation when Bitterroot singled me out.

I said it's how we roll, Private Kowalski. Not you.

Group laughter.

So I stood on the front bumper of a troop carrier and read aloud from the back of the can. *Warning! Contains butanol, ethyl acetate, xylene and toluene! Extremely flammable! Eye and skin irritant! Always use safety goggles! Always use solvent-resistant gloves! Vapor harmful if inhaled!* Then, already sweating in the immense heat, I held my gloveless hand open in the universal WTF gesture.

Problem solved, Private Kowalski, Bitterroot said, and slapped a wire brush in my palm. Don't inhale, and don't smoke. And make sure to keep your hands clean. He was big and blocky and pink, with an incongruously high voice like he'd been sucking on helium.

It's Private Kovacs, Master Sergeant Bitterroot, I said, trying without luck to make my voice deeper. The vast penetrat-
ing desert heat had already dried out my throat so that I was
rasping like a forty-year smoker, like someone who'd swallowed
sandpaper.

And what about this? I said. Damages automotive paints?

That stumped him, for a second. Sweetpea had already broken out his pocket dictionary and begun reading, and the rest of
them had their eyes shut. Then Bitterroot shrugged and ducked
down with the others, sheltering from the desert sun in the blue
shade spreading out to the east of the truck. The glare from the
hood was blinding, so I looked back up over the sea of vehicles I
was supposed to start cleaning, trembling in the heat waves like
they were melting. I felt like I was: my face flash-fried, my skin
scorched and sliding off my molten bones.

We got our orders, he said from the shade. Now you got
yours.

Sweatpea piped up with his squeaky voice. Indubitably, he
said, though I wasn't sure if he was reading aloud from the dictionary or just commenting on the appropriateness of Sergeant
Bitterroot's order.

Hummers, tanks, Strykers, APCs, artillery pieces too. A
half-dozen gleaming Beamers off in one corner—the confisca-
tory powers of the Coalition Authority, no doubt—and all of
them tagged with graffiti that it was now my job to scrub off. I
figured if I could do one an hour, it would only take about a bil-
lion years.

Master Sergeant Bitterroot, I said.

He took his time responding. What, Private Kowalski. The
way he said it, it wasn't really a question. He sounded almost
asleep.

Private Kovacs requests permission to speak, Master
Sergeant.

Speak.

Being a replacement sucks, Master Sergeant.

Just figuring that out now, Private?

Once when the firing stopped on the artillery range—Bedouins were herding their camels across it, a common sight I'd been told, but still worth taking in—Bitterroot didn't hear me spraying solvent or scraping metal. He called out, Private Kowalski?

Dwell time, Master Sergeant Bitterroot, I said. Says it on the can.

Dwell time is what we're doing, he said. Get your ass in gear.

So I did. A lot was just swearing or hometown stuff or biblical references, some was seasonal or political—Merry Christmas, TONY BLIAR, Saddam Sucks—and favorite teams got coverage: Sox and Yankees, Celts and Lakers, though there were some mad-ass taggers—Sheff had been particularly active, and his throwies were pretty dope—but most of it was crap, and of course gang signs. You had your Latin Kings and Crips and Bloods, Gangster Disciples and Vice Lords, some Florencia 13s and 38th Streeters, even a few P-Stones, Norteños and Simon City Royals. Three KKKers that I could scope out, and one Aryan Nation. They'd all thrown up their signs. C's up next to a B's down, painted over with a B's up, C's down. MOBs, three-dot dog paws, 031, five-pointed stars, six-pointed stars, tridents upright and inverted, crescent moons. So many gangs, and some I didn't even recognize. 150%, MS, 13, IGC. Who the hell were they? All learning to be better warriors. Jesus. We were in for it once all this was done and all those newly-trained warriors hit the streets.

And me, scrubbing the shit all alone. While I watched, the paint bubbled up as if the metal were coming to a boil, Sheff

being wiped from the planet one throw at a time, and I wondered if it was the toluene that made my eyes water, the xylene
that burned my skin. And who knew what the butanol and acetate were doing to my lungs and balls, which respectively felt
banded and bound? I pictured myself as a forty-year-old dad
wheeling around an oxygen tank and kids with fins. Yeah, I was
in the war, can't you see?

This silence I felt before I heard it: another flock of camels—is that what they call it?—marching across the firing range,
Bedouins urging them on. The strange thing was that some of
this group of Bedouins were driving some of this group of camels in flatbeds. A relief corps? Who knew? But the silence was
why I heard the question, asked by a roving corporal.

Anyone here ever milk a cow?

I waggled the slimed-over scrub brush in the air. Stupid, I
realized, the second I did it—the rule is, wait for someone else
to do it and see what happens—and lowered my arm too late.
Who'd have thought a high-school field trip could get you in so
much trouble?

So early the next morning I'm at a forward operating base,
another replacement standing next to another sergeant,
Christianson, big and dark as a plum this time, and he's pointing out a guy who could be Saddam's younger brother leaving the village two hundred yards off to walk in our direction, same hair, same mustache, same swagger—though at
this distance eyes and mouth are just dots—and dressed in a
sky-blue track suit. The world was greener here, north of the
Euphrates, crops in the field, fig trees, palms. The cow was
halfway between us.

The sarge sighted Saddam's mini-me with his gun. That's
him, he said.

I realized the game: spook the newbie. I decided to play the newbie who couldn't be spooked. Christianson had a rich deep voice and a Pennsylvania accent. You from Pittsburgh, Staff Sergeant Christianson? I asked.

You don't need to know that, Private Newbie. If they capture you they'll make you talk before they cut your balls off.

I heard laughter behind us.

Seriously, Newbie, he said. Last a week and I'll tell you.

I could see where this was going, so I gave in. So, how can you tell he's the spotter?

Phone.

Lots of people have phones. Look over there. I pointed at the village's cluster of low, mud-colored buildings, where knots of people—men, women, kids—were watching us, half of them on phones.

No, the sarge said not looking away. He's the spotter. Trust me.

His gun barrel was following him. Mortars? I said.

Mortars. They came in yesterday, and earlier this morning. The same guy.

How do you know?

Track suit.

Lots of guys dressed in track suits here.

Yeah. But how many of them are sky blue? And how many of those are walking around former minefields near a FOB? And stay there when mortars start falling? Everyone else ran away.

He dropped him with a single shot, flat on his back across three furrows. The echo bounced off the village walls and everyone vanished like they'd been sucked into the earth. Not even any rising dust to mark their passage.

The spotter's boots were crossed at the ankles as if he were taking a nap, the hobnails glinting. I made myself think about what Christianson had just said instead of what I'd just seen.

A former minefield? I said. How former?

Don't worry. We cleared it. See those feathers?

I did, now, thousands of them tangled in the grass and shoots, flickering light and dark as the wind moved over them like they were trying to signal something. *This is important,* I kept thinking, but I couldn't figure out why.

He tapped the wall of the building we were in. This was a chicken ranch when we got there. Hundreds of hungry, angry chickens.

That explained the smell of bird shit.

Christianson said, We chased them out in the field.

The chickens? I said. They blew up the mines? That explained the smell of rotting meat.

Yep.

But chickens don't weigh much, I said.

Not individually, but in aggregate.

He had to be BS-ing me. I mean, they weren't going to send one of their own—even a replacement—across a possible mine-field for fresh milk, were they?

Why don't you bring the cow closer? I said.

We're not supposed to steal the cow. The locals would think we were. Rules of Engagement. No looting. And if it was near us and someone shot it they'd say it was us. So we're renting it.

Renting?

Six bucks a day. Not a bad deal. She wanted to sell it to us for five hundred dollars. She gives us info too. Told us we'd get mortared today, and we did. And it's good for Iraqi morale. Shows we're not just here to blow up things. Hearts and minds.

Not mine, Staff Sergeant Christianson.

We own your heart and mind, Kovacs. We don't have to win them. He turned back to the cow. Besides, he said, it draws them out. The spotter thought standing behind the cow hid him.

Draws us out too.

Not us. You. Here, he said, and held up a green plastic bucket. Fill 'er up.

I wanted to put this off as long as possible. Staff Sergeant

Christianson, why is the captain doing this? How come fresh milk is so important?

Strictly NTK, Kovacs, and you're not in the Need-To-Know sphere.

That wasn't going anywhere, so I decided to draw on my vast bovine experience. Cows like routine, I said. What time did you milk her yesterday?

Zero-nine-hundred.

I glanced at my watch. Fifteen minutes still.

Christianson gave me the moron look. They've got to wait to get another spotter, Private Kovacs, he said. My guess is he'll be here in less than ten minutes. Get moving. You'll be fine if you hurry. But if I'm wrong, or if they bring out a new one, just duck your head and make a noise like a mushroom.

All the way across the field the bullseye on my forehead seemed to deepen and expand. I tried not to think about the spotter as I walked, how, if I'd been standing next to him when he was shot, the shot would have popped like a champagne cork, or how the wind was tugging at his pant cuffs now. Instead my mind wandered to the Dragunov sniper rifle. I wished I'd paid more attention to the lectures. What was its range, 800 meters? Someone could hit me from the opposite side of the village at that distance. A flash suppressor, corrosion resistant, those I remembered. What useless shit we fill our brains with. Of course, if he was out there, he was hoping to empty mine of everything. The spotter's crossed ankles still threw me, like he was out for a lazy morning. But there might be other spotters. The bullseye moved. Up to my helmet, where it became a Red Cross emblem.

Even that early the heat shimmered like I was walking in gas fumes, and my boots weighed a thousand pounds each; I was slogging through warm wax. I lost three pounds of sweat just getting there. No stool, so I'd have to crouch, but at least I'd be hidden, except for my legs. Ho, Sandy, I said, and patted her flank. She eyed me, then turned back to the business of eating.

I didn't want to communicate my nerves to her—cows can be finicky, and finicky cows take longer to milk out—so I squatted quickly but smoothly, like I did this every day. Behind me, from the hut, came an annoying beeping sound. She turned her head toward it and I patted her again, told her it was all right. Nothing for you to worry about, I said, pushing her head straight. Means they're playing computer games.

She turned back again so I went to plan B, pulling salt from my pocket and letting her sandpaper tongue rough up my hand. Then I upended the bucket, spanked the bottom, righted it and wiped it down with my bandana, settled it under her, and rested my head on her dusty flank. Breathed. That pleasant cow scent. Must be the same the world over.

I'd carried a wet rag with me, over my shoulder, and the rag had soaked through my uniform. I lifted it and cleaned her udder, swollen and tight. Teats in my palms, thumb and forefinger squeezing the top, closing my fingers sequentially until the first warm spray splattered and foamed against the plastic. I still had it. Then my right hand, then again with my left, shifting from teat to teat. Good size teats too, all four working, and she wasn't a dancer, which was nice, though she did swat me with her tail— the new guy, the wrong time—and when she let down her milk she let down her shit too, giant warm brown pancakes which the flies were on before they hit the ground. Tinny music was playing somewhere in the distance, something Arabic with what sounded like a busted banjo. I found myself squeezing in rhythm with it. My nose was dripping, my face wet, and I was going to wipe my nose on my shoulder to keep the snot from dropping into the milk, but then I thought, *Screw it*. The captain could drink my snot with his warm milk if he wanted to put me out here.

In a few minutes the udder was noticeably softer and the pail foaming and full. I patted her again and thanked her for the milk but didn't stand immediately, as it might be the last time I ever did.

Fuck it, I said, and stood. I wasn't going to run. They were all lined up to watch me, I could see them. I wasn't going to give them a show. The pail was heavy and sloshy.

The spotter was gone. Who'd come for him? And how had I not heard it? His boots had left drag marks perpendicular to the furrowed field, so exact they might have been laid out by an engineer. My elbows felt dislocated by the time I got back.

Martinez was shoving a cleaning patch through the barrel with a cleaning rod. He had *Prada* tattooed on his lower eyelid, and through his glasses it looked like it was on the lens. But it was the five-pointed star inked on the underside of his left wrist that caught my attention; that and the left earring and the rolled-up left pant leg. A true people person.

Hey, I said. They didn't really herd the chickens out into that field, did they?

Around his lit cigarette, he said, Which field?

That minefield?

It ain't no minefield.

I felt my shoulders straighten. Nah, I knew that, I said. But why all the feathers?

He looked up at me at last. My hands were still adrenaline-jumpy, so I tucked them under my arms.

There was a chicken farm. We drove 'em out when we cleared the building.

They blow up?

No. Mortars got most of 'em. We probably shot the rest.

What a mess.

No shit.

He bent to inspect the cleaning patch for copper fouling, the cigarette smoke drifting up over his helmet. It smelled good, but he wasn't going to offer me one. All replacements are mendicants, for food, for material, for attention and conversation. Friendship most of all. So I asked.

He one-handed the pack from his pocket, shook one loose, extended it. I had to ask for the light too. It made me cough.

Still concentrating on the barrel, he said, First one?

Yeah.

Bad habit.

One I hope to have for a long time. I inhaled, coughed again, and said, Martinez, tell me. Why does the captain have such a jones for milk?

I don't know, Martinez said, but rumor is he's got hemorrhoids.

Hemorrhoids? How does the milk help that? What's he do, soak his ass in the bucket?

Martinez continued cleaning his gun. Don't know that either, he said. Captain's not in the habit of talking to me about his butt.

Nothing to do but be out with it, so I said, Lemme have your paints.

I ain't got no paints.

Bullshit, I said. I seen 'em.

Actually, I hadn't, but he seemed a likely target. And the gamble was worth it if it meant I didn't have to be a walking bullseye.

Fuck off, Newbie.

All right, I said. Fine. But I only got half a pail today. Sandy's not happy.

Who's Sandy?

The cow. Someone's got to hold her. When I tell Christianson, who you think he'll send? You're on burn duty, for shit's sake.

And he was; he smelled of it, gasoline, smoke, burned paper and singed fur. Trash and dead dogs, here—the perfect place to hide IEDs—but back at camp it had probably been shit. Once you got tagged for something like that, it was hard to get off.

Be smart, I said.

I am, he said, taking out his bore brush, oiling it, and bending again to his task. You don't see me talking to you, do you?

How could a single afternoon feel like a month? It did. Fifteen minutes before I had to go again, I lay with my head on my pack and my helmet tilted over my eyes. It was a way of not pacing, of making it seem I couldn't care less about what I was about to do.

But not pacing gave me time to think, and this is what I thought repeatedly, like a tongue finding a sore tooth again and again: that the most technologically advanced civilization in the history of earth had gathered up me and thousands of others, trained us and brought us here at God knows what sort of taxpayer expense and parceled us out to lie in this patch of dirt. One of its drones could fly over the city and see a man lying on the roof and not know if he was dead or sleeping or planning to rise up once the drone was gone and flip aside the rug beside him to reveal a sniper rifle. Nor could it tell, watching me, if *I* was dead or alive, and if alive, sleeping or wide awake, filled with the normal terrors of a new soldier plus one extra: that walk across the naked field to the too-obvious cow. Civilization maximus, reaching back in time to produce our oldest prototypes, hunters and gatherers. I was already tired of being the gatherer.

Someone kicked my boots and I pushed up my helmet. Martinez, outlined against the dropping sun.

He didn't get shot, you know, he said.

Who?

He nodded toward Sandy. The milker you replaced. Aryan Nation. They'd been investigating him for months. Turned out he'd been shipping home flak jackets. Lots of 'em.

You don't have to worry, I said. I'm not A.N.

What are you?

I'm not anything.

Got that right. Nothing, and not for long, neither.

I didn't say anything. He hadn't come by just to give me that news, but pushing it wouldn't help; he had to be ready. At last he hawked, spit, looked around; then he squatted and flipped open his pack. Three gold lids and one black. He reached for a gold.

Got to be black, I said.

What's it for? It's my last one.

I held my out my hand. Give it up.

He mumbled something—I didn't listen too closely—but smacked it against my palm, and I hid it under my flak jacket, wondering the whole way out (carrying two buckets this time): if they shot me and the Kevlar stopped it, would the shock wave be enough to blow up the can? Science experiments you don't want to be part of. My heart was pounding so hard I thought the can would pop out anyway, and I kept striding into my lengthening shadow, never quite catching it, though I tried.

In addition to the can under my Kevlar, I'd tucked a note in my pants pocket. *Dear Mom and Dad, You'll be sorry if you get this, though not half as sorry as me. But you should know the truth, and I doubt the military would tell you, so here it is: I'm probably the first person in recorded history killed in combat by a CO's hemorrhoids.*

They'd never get it, but it felt good to write. A tinny voice came over the tinny loudspeaker, supposedly the muezzin calling the faithful to prayer, though for all I knew he was chanting, *Shoot The Infidel!* It didn't help that everyone in the village disappeared at once, or that we wouldn't get new info from the cow's owner until the next day. I'd asked Christianson about that.

Not till the morning, he said. We don't want to endanger her, Private Newbie. Showing up too often would make people suspect her.

Don't want to endanger *her*? I said.

He rested his gun barrel against his shoulder and looked at me, for the first time. She didn't sign up for this, he said.

He had a point.

The cow looked browner in the fading light. She spread her rear legs for greater balance as soon as she saw me. Must have been sore, which made sense, since I left her bag partially taut in the morning, and she milked easy, even without the salt offering, though this time the milk gave off a slight oniony smell; there must have been wild ones about. The captain probably wasn't going to enjoy this batch as much unless he liked omelets, but I filled all of one bucket and most of the second, deflating her bag until it wrinkled.

It was near dark when I finished, and once I balanced out the pails I put them behind me—upwind, since the captain might be able to abide onion-flavored milk, but paint-flavored milk had no chance of flying—and reached under my vest for the can. Then the weirdest thing happened. At the very first touch of paint to cow she began to tremble, her entire hide to twitch, as if she knew what I was doing, and I felt bad. Horrible. I rested my hand on her, hoping my touch would calm her, felt her breathing and shaking against my palm, patted her flank, leaned my forearm against her bony hip, whispered words of encouragement.

It's all right girl, I said. You've got nothing to fear.

But when she turned to look at me with those knowing eyes, I stopped; it was like lying to a baby. Stopped whispering, that is, but I didn't stop painting. She didn't stop trembling and twitching but she didn't move; the knowing seemed to freeze her. She also gave off a new, acrid smell, but I told myself that maybe that was just the paint mixing with her own scent.

I'd done the camp side first, shielding it from view with my body, but it was dark enough now that I could go round to the other side, and I did. If anyone asked, I was going to say it was prep for tomorrow, soothing her, important after the day's last milking. A few lights were on in the village, none in the camp, just the last palmy outlines of trees visible on the western horizon. The moment seemed momentous, and it wouldn't have been right not to mark it, so I bowed my head and prayed.

Dear Lord, I mumbled. I offer you this cow on the altar of my private dreams, my desire to stay alive. Let me have today and tomorrow my daily bread, and forgive me my selfishness, as I forgive others who selfishly wish my death in return, and lead them not into the temptation to kill me, but deliver me from their evil, and them from mine.

I paused there, thinking of adding more to it, about how He had given us dominion over the beasts in the fields, and about how my country had a part in this, her country as well, fate and history too; but then I realized that their role in all of this would be up to Him to decide. So, to finish off, I said, I'm making my offering in full knowledge that I alone am responsible for my part in it, for wishing neither the power nor the glory, but only to survive, forever and ever, Amen.

Then I picked up the full heavy buckets and started back. This time I couldn't switch hands on a single pail, so it was a long walk across that darkening field. The last light seemed to disappear all at once, so fast I thought I'd gone blind or been shot or that some giant unseen hand had clamped a wok lid down on the bowl of the sky, and of course that made everything worse.

I had to go slow in order not to stumble but I stumbled anyway, moving on through the dark toward an unknown destination, which I realized was like all of us, though with luck for most that final destination isn't a bunch of soldiers holding guns. And I felt the villagers pouring out behind me, a whole host of them, sneaking up with guns to shoot me with, knives to slit my throat. I knew they were there and I knew they weren't too; each time my boots skidded over the loamy furrows, giving off a whispery sound, I heard them whispering, letting out their pent-up fury, at us, at themselves, at those elements among them they despised. They hated us, I realized, so much that they came to get the spotter who they hated too, for bringing danger and death down on them, but they hated us worse—they didn't leave him out there for us to gloat over, to feed the superiority of our pity. Twenty-eight million whispers are really loud, even if they're not really there.

I became irrationally afraid that everyone had pulled out and left me behind—they were damn good on light and noise discipline—and by the time I made it back to the chicken shed my arms and elbows were in agony; I felt like I'd been hung from them. I tripped right at the end and almost lost it all but Christianson was there to stand me up.

I huffed out my thanks and he said, Not a problem.

I gave up the buckets and knelt to catch my breath and said, The captain must like his milk.

Christianson said, He does. He sniffed it, stood. Though I don't know about this batch. Want some?

No. I'm lactose intolerant.

He was still laughing minutes later. Which was just as well; it prevented him from asking what the hell I'd been doing at the end, and at that point I didn't think I could lie about it.

I pulled first watch, which was uneventful, except for the blue flare that took a long time to burn out and that made me duck my head like a turtle. Sandy didn't even twitch when it went off; instead she stood looking two-dimensional, like a cut-out of a cow someone had put in a field for laughs. I crashed in my ranger grave, which no one had helped me dig, and looked up at the stars. I was out before I even had a sense that they were moving.

At zero five-hundred, I was up with everyone else. If the dark had come fast, the light came up even faster, the sky brightening from indigo to baby blue in seconds and the sun up all at once and scorching like it was launched out of a toaster. Sandy's long shadow reached toward us, as did the palms' and the village's, and I realized that the site must have been chosen in the afternoon when the sun would have blinded the bad guys. But like a lot of things that look good at night, the decision didn't seem so smart in the morning. A group of soldiers clustered by the wall, scoping the field.

Who the fuck would tag a cow? someone said. Six heads swiveled as one to Martinez, who in turn turned to me, but I knew he wasn't going to give me up. His paint, his rival's sign, no way he wanted to step into that.

Besides, I was looking at the cow, the six-pointed stars clearly visible on her flank. Three gallons a day was a good amount; someone was going to miss her.

That's a gang sign, someone said, isn't it? That star?

Black Gangster Disciples, I piped up, helpfully.

It's also Jewish, Christianson said.

As if on cue, the shot came right after, though none of us picked up the muzzle flash. Her rear legs buckled, she bellowed once, then thumped over onto her side, throwing up a dust cloud.

Asshole, Christianson said. I wasn't sure who he was referring to. Burn duty, Martinez, he said.

Come on, Sarge. It wasn't me. And besides, he's not near a road.

She, Christianson said. And she might be before long, since we're pulling out. And then someone else will have to deal with it.

I pushed forward. I'll go with him, I said.

Okay. Christianson seemed to think it was out of feelings for the cow. He sent a squad with us to set up a perimeter. The gas cans were lighter than the milk pails, but the cow took forever to burn. Twice when the flames died down I stepped forward and splashed her good; the second time the flames shot up so fast they singed my eyebrows, but I wanted it over with.

Anybody got cornbread? Teets asked, breathing in the smoke. That's some fine barbeque.

She was still smoldering when it was time to leave, blackened, stiffened, reduced, but still there; the truth isn't easy to burn.

Kovacs, Christianson said. You ride with me. Martinez, you and Teets are with Spenser.

When I got in, Christianson said, Malvern. Not too far from Philly.

Nice part of the country, I said. Tell me, is Harry Teets his real name?

Yeah. Can you believe it? Nice parents, huh?

I sat in the Hummer, joyfully watching the unfamiliar landscape slip by, glad to be alive, but feeling bad for Harry Teets. Newbie-dom was a finite thing—someone else was bound to come along eventually—and you could sometimes get past being a shit burner, but your name? You could never climb out from under something like that. That was as indubitably fixed as the North Star.

The Only Appearance of Rice

They were all the same: as children they had gone with fishing poles to catch dreams, never fish, or perhaps they had hoped to catch fish and had a talent for dreams instead. The lures for one, it turned out, were the same as for the other.

He remembered how excited he was when he ran home to tell his mother, the string of dreams bouncing behind him, and his surprise at her reaction, burying her face in a bag of rice. Even through it he heard her sobs.

Grains clung to her face when she raised it.

The Wind, It Blows Forever

The wind gusts, taking away the minister's words, and I'm in the hallway with Mark, just after my first brush with Andrea. He seems excited to tell me the news—is shouting over the screen door banging in the wind—that I've been elected first to die.

I won't pretend the news didn't startle me. I said, Why?

He looked puzzled. The door blew open, letting in the smell of salt water, the bright bitter air, slammed shut. Probably your driving, he said.

Passing that car going uphill around a turn? I said.

He nodded.

I paused. You know, I said, I've always wondered. Where were those nuns going at 2:00 a.m., and why was the music in their car so loud?

He had no answer. At last he said, And your father's car.

I'd driven his small blue Renault seventy miles an hour backward, all four doors open, between two parked trucks in a snowy, darkened parking lot because Mark had bet me I couldn't. I could and did, though I nearly destroyed the car when all four doors were torn off by truck mirrors that extended farther into space than I'd imagined. This was February in New Hampshire, and the next day I had to drive three hundred and fifty miles home with no doors during a snowstorm to explain to my dad why his car was suddenly a new kind of convertible.

What were you elected? I said to Mark.

His tan face broke into a goofy smile. First to go crazy.

•

Now the minister's talking about life after death. I don't believe it; never did. Mark didn't either. That week, we talked a lot about the hereafter, how the here and now seemed so much better. It was a group vacation beach-rental, all couples except for me because my girlfriend had broken up with me days before. The jealous type. You'll probably like Andrea more than me, anyway, she'd said. I liked Andrea less.

We met in the kitchen, she squatting in front of the open fridge as if God might be in there and she would see Him if only she remained still. After a proper wait I cleared my throat. She turned to face me, the long black ponytail sliding over her browned back.

Andrea, I said, saying it like it was spelled.

Ahn-DRAY-uh, she corrected me, and turned away without another word, the ponytail rocking back across those wing-like clavicles. I thought of reaching over her, but it was our first meeting and I didn't want to start things off on the wrong foot—something she evidently couldn't care less about—so I pitched my voice to sound as friendly as possible. Hey, do you think you could hand me a beer?

Get your own when I'm done.

That's all right, I said, my voice still friendly as I reached over her. I'll save myself the trouble and get it now.

An hour later I met her boyfriend, wearing three polo shirts one over the other, the collars standing straight up. You're the jerk who couldn't wait for a beer, Jeff said. You an alcoholic?

No, I said, making a joke of it. Just an asshole.

Got that right, he said.

There was no need to watch out for him. He and Andrea were so obnoxious that it became a kind of informal game to see if we could piss them off, which turned out to be remarkably easy. Mispronouncing her name, and, in his case, asking,

Where'd you go to school again? That turned both of their faces red, since he'd announced the first day that the smartest people in America had always gone to Amherst.

They never did dishes, at the local bars they disappeared when it was their turn to buy a round, they let others do the shopping and came back from their beach walks after the groceries had been unloaded to make a show of producing their wallets and asking what their share was; they didn't want anyone to think they weren't pulling their weight. The night it was their turn to cook a communal dinner they brought back two buckets of KFC and a miniature tub of lukewarm mashed potatoes. No gravy, they said, since they wanted to charge them extra for it. Could we believe it? We could.

The wind blows over an entire row of foldable chairs—we'd hoped for a bigger crowd, but didn't expect it—and a few of us busy ourselves righting them from among the graves, hair and ties whipping our faces. Good cover for red eyes, if anyone wants it. The minister talks on, hand clamped on the Bible page.

Our last day on that vacation, I woke from a nap with tight skin and a growling stomach. Food supplies were running low— Jeff and Andrea had promised to run to the grocery store for snacks, but hadn't—and after poking through the nearly empty fridge and cabinets I found a plateful of brownies hidden under a cake pan. I ate a half dozen, washing them down with beers. On the porch Mark and Sarah were napping in the hammock, and I woke them to share the bounty.

Not very good, I told them, but a hell of a lot better with lager.

We ate in companionable silence, staring out at the glittering ocean and listening to the steady creak of the hammock, the complaining gulls, the waves smashing against rocks. The air smelled vinegary—rotting seaweed—which, in my present mood, was peculiarly pleasant.

Jeff and Andrea swearing in the kitchen and throwing around pots and pans ruined our reverie. They boiled out of the house and marched up to us.

Lose something? I asked.

Yes, Andrea said. Another one of these.

Her mistake was holding the plate of brownies toward us. Mark was big but very quick, and he took the plate from her before she had a chance to react, then held it behind his back, where Sarah and I began stuffing them into our mouths.

Hey! Andrea yelled, but Mark wouldn't let her by him on the narrow porch, and by the time Jeff climbed down and ran around behind us we'd eaten the entire batch.

Do you have any idea how much those brownies cost? Andrea said.

I still had a mouthful so I shook my head no.

You stupid son of a bitch, Jeff said. I hope you gag on them.

I was about to, but after chugging the last beer I was fine.

Don't think I'm going to, pardner, I said. But for what it's worth, your brownies weren't any good, anyway, so I don't know what you're bitching about.

They aren't *supposed* to be good, Andrea said. She was shaking. They're hash brownies.

Hash? I said.

And were you going to share them? Sarah asked.

Of course, Jeff said, but he couldn't look her in the eye. The wind was so strong that week. His foolish red hair, it stood straight out.

After an awkward silence, I said, Well, they don't seem to be working, so whatever you paid for that hash, you should get your money back.

•

What I learned on my summer vacation that year was that hash brownies don't take effect for a long time. Also, ingested in sufficient quantities, they simply make time disappear. After eating, the next thing I remember is buying lobsters at the lobster pound, a three-mile walk from our house. I remember nothing of the walk back. I do recall Mark and Sarah and me holding a rowboat over a long fissure in the rocks, me at the bow and them at the stern, the three of us giggling as we tried to steer toward the waterline, the lobsters in the silty bilge water scrabbling about as we did. We planned to free them. Sarah had a big smile and dark tiny eyes and that big blond hair, which gave her face a faint yellow cast, and when she smiled I got the idea that she'd been the inspiration for the yellow Happy Face logo, which made me laugh so much my stomach hurt.

Then we were out on the water, twenty yards offshore, aiming for a small island, all of us declaring very loudly that neither Jeff nor Andrea were really that bad. Now and then one of the lobsters, their claws stupidly freed from their blue rubber-band restraints before we were ready to pitch them overboard, pinched our bare ankles and toes. Sarah, with the big smiling yellow Happy Face on top of her big shoulders, looked happier than ever.

Then the boat was gone and I was up on the tin porch roof by myself in the dark, lying stretched out on my stomach, the tin cool beneath me, watching the water surge and splash against the rocks below. The roofline was nearly to the water; if I jumped far enough I could make it.

I hung my head over the clogged gutter and bellowed until the entire house was outside in the spotlighted yard. Then I stood up.

Ready? I yelled.

Ready! came the roar, and I ran like my ass was on fire, feet pounding across that tin roof (so loud!) until I threw myself off at top speed.

My traitorous balls had worked themselves halfway up to my shoulders when time stopped. I could see everything so clearly, phosphorescent drops of water caught mid-bounce off the glistening rocks, the wind in one woman's canary yellow blouse, the dark open mouths of Mark and Sarah, Jeff and Andrea leaning forward to be the first witnesses to where I splattered. *If this kills me,* I thought, *it will be one hell of a last view.*

Then time returned and the rocks rushed toward me. Water, rocks, rocks, water—which would I hit? *And even if it was water, would it be deep enough?* I should have checked that out first; but with a rush of exhilaration I knew I was in the clear, that nothing but water lay beneath me. Then a gust of wind slammed into my chest.

The wind's crazy here now too, shredding the minister's words. Don't criticize me, it's the weather that's always melodramatic at these things.

He's into the formulaic part, ashes to ashes, dust to dust, so I can follow along, and really, I can't blame him. What can you do? Someone lives, then dies, and you gather with swollen eyes and shattered hearts to mourn him. The form's a given: darkness to begin with, darkness at the end, with luck some light in between. The issue is what that light consists of, and that's a mystery that even those closest to someone can't often fathom.

Take me, for instance. I squeeze Andrea's hand and she smiles at me. I'd got over thinking she was an ass and she'd forgiven me for being one. She appeared every day in the hospital and drove me to rehab for my broken legs. Lying in that bed, without telling her, I swore that my election would never come true, that my rooftop jump—not my various stupidities with cars, not my tumble through a plate-glass window, not stabbing myself accidentally in the thigh with my own lockblade—would be the dumbest thing I'd ever done.

Or take Mark, who collected both his honor and mine in such surprisingly swift fashion and who is now flying on through the dark. I look at the sparse crowd, not surprised to note Sarah's absence—schizophrenia scares off all but the stoutest—though it is a bit surprising to see Jeff here, far stouter than either Mark or I had imagined. Then again Andrea and I had attended his commitment ceremony to Aaron in Boston, and perhaps that had swayed him.

I stand, rest one hand on the polished wooden coffin— warmed by the sun—and say my silent last goodbye to Mark. Then, with Andrea beside me, I turn away, and we lean forward into the conquering wind.

Hotei

Because the Urgent Care cubicles afford no privacy, I know the woman on my left—though not a diabetic—has a terrible rash covering her stomach and thighs, and the woman on my right is miscarrying. Blood, cramps.

How frequent?

Right now, she gasps.

Have you miscarried before?

No. My first.

My turn to answer the questions comes and I tell the woman, Thank you, but really, I'm fine.

Your finger doesn't hurt, ma'am?

No, I say, and bend it without breathing. It's really okay, I say.

Outside, I move the car, prop my hand on the steering wheel and Scotch-tape the finger to the next one, careful not to take my eyes off the two entrances. It's warm, so I don't worry about running out of gas—I should have listened to my husband, who tells me to keep a full tank in case of emergencies—or about being too cold, though for that I do have a blanket.

Three hours, I think; she'll wait an hour, given the crowded room, then she'll be on the examining table, feet up, doctor between her legs, some mifepristone if the miscarriage wasn't complete, Methergine if it was, a suitable waiting period, then half an hour or so to check out. The nurse will make suggestions:

watch for surging hormones, for depression, for pain. She'll give advice too: the big pads will not catch all the blood.

I don't let myself sleep in case I'm wrong. After forty-five minutes my finger worsens—it's certainly broken—so I hunt down an Advil by touch and chew it, not liking to swallow pills, eyes watering at the bitter taste, and after I loosen my finger and retape it, she comes out. At first I don't recognize her in the pink raincoat. It's no surprise she's early; she was only two months pregnant. Head down, which I remember, taking her time, which I don't. I'd hurried, afraid everyone around could intuit my flaw. Maybe it's the five-month difference.

She turns onto Studebaker Drive and I follow her, an expert now at night driving. For months after my first miscarriage I went grocery shopping past midnight, telling my husband I was too busy with work to shop at more normal times, but really I knew I'd see almost no women with babies then—women who angered me—though when some new mother did appear in the bright aisles I followed her and her competent cervix discreetly, turning one lane farther up, matching my pace to her imagined one, staring into opened freezers as if actually choosing between Stouffer's and Mrs. Paul's. Strange, I knew, but also unavoidable, that self-lacerating pull. I felt dirty and defective, secretly dipped in sin, and wondered why the whole world was a tuxedo and I a pair of brown shoes; everyone but me could have a baby.

She pulls into an Indian restaurant, which is hard to believe. After two minutes I follow her in, wondering how she keeps from throwing up: stinging curry, fried rice, the clammy scent of steamed vegetables; after each miscarriage, my nose had always been extrasensitive. Lose a baby and become a bloodhound—quite the tradeoff.

She's taken a table in the back and I wish I'd come in sooner, having no idea whether she's ordered a little or a lot. I sit side-

ways to keep her in my peripheral vision. By the register, surrounded by offerings of bright oranges, sagging samosas, and
tangled cellophane noodles, squats a fat smiling Buddha, though
it's a turbaned Sikh who stands behind the counter, stroking his
beard. She makes a call, laughing once, which she shouldn't
do—no reason to tempt the gods—and when the waiter comes
and asks me something in indecipherable English I point at two
things on the menu and smile.

It must be a sympathetic reaction that makes me gag when
the food arrives, but I make myself eat, trying to forget my ach-
ing hand, which the waiter notices. I can't quite make out his
accented English, so I smile and nod again, and three minutes
later he's back with a roll of electric tape and a pair of scissors.
My blush burns.

Without asking, he cuts the Scotch Tape from my hand and
unrolls a length of electric tape. I try not to move the fingers—
if it doesn't hurt too badly, I should be able to keep my com-
posure—and as he's taping them back together the woman gets
up, carrying her plate. Is she coming to eat with me?

She doesn't even look at our commotion, instead she
crouches before the Buddha, lays her plate at his feet and rubs his
belly, resting her hand there while she closes her eyes. Done, she
stands, puts a twenty on the counter and leaves. Food untouched,
I see. Had she called her husband and followed his suggestions?

My own food feels sticky in my mouth, turns over in my
stomach, but I will not throw up here. I thank the waiter, who
bows and backs away.

I should have sat closer, so I could have heard her conversation. If it had been her husband—she wore a wedding ring—
why wasn't he with her? Perhaps he was traveling, as Rob had
been for my third. He had been there for my first. That time I'd
reached into the toilet thinking, *Here she is, my baby*, and Rob
tried to stop me, scooping from my cupped palms what turned
out to be a large rubbery clot of blood.

•

The door opens again and she's back. I turn to look at the table for her purse and she stops beside me. Here, she says, holding out a white paper bag. I've got some surgical tape. It'll work better than that.

Oh, thank you, I say.

When I don't take the bag, she says, It's okay. It's from the Urgent Care place down the road.

Don't you need it? I say, then exclaim in surprise when I glimpse the rose tattooed on the underside of her wrist.

It's all right, she says, misinterpreting my shock. A brief smile. Tape won't solve my problem.

I hope it's nothing serious, I say, and take the bag.

She breathes in and I can feel her mind working, the telepathy of the malformed. If my finger didn't hurt so much, I'd laugh at my own foolishness. She exhales, says at last, Miscarriage.

I look deep inside the open bag as if the words to soothe her might be printed on the bottom, shake it so the tape and pads bounce and switch positions. I'm so sorry, I say.

No, it's better, I think. My body must have rejected it for a reason.

I glance up. But how can we ever know what our body's reasons are?

We can't. Ever. No matter what the doctors say. But I'm praying that next time it will be better.

She turns away without me telling her that prayers might soon turn bitter on her tongue. What would be the point? She'll learn that lesson soon enough, along with others: that the due date will be brutal, that pity is crushing, that well meant words from fools will wound the most. *It must have been defective. God had a plan. It wasn't really a baby.* Words I've probably spoken once or twice myself.

I watch her go. The waiter asks (I think), Is she your sister?

No.

Who?

It comes out in a rush, and I don't care if he understands. She had a rose tattoo, I say. My baby's name was going to be Rose.

He smiles and nods.

A nurse said I should get a tattoo of her on my foot, so I'd always remember.

I stand and say, As if I'd ever forget.

I pay the silent Sikh, resisting the urge to touch the Buddha's fat belly for luck, and pause at the door; her red brake lights wink off and her small blue car accelerates away in the dark. I turn, kneel, lay my wet face against the Buddha's smooth swollen stomach. It's *in* there, I think. What I want, what I need, what will make me whole. I don't care that they've gathered around me now, the two waiters with nothing to do and the tiny curious busboy, the scowling Sikh with his bushy black beard. I shift, pull up my blouse, press my bare skin to the Buddha's cold metal, the swollen bronze belly warming as my hollow warm one touches it, as if it's coming to life.

This will work, I tell myself. *It will. I promise you.*

Why I Like the Blues

The code was a thousand numbers long, easy to write, easier to break. Walpeter sat at his desk, bored by the coders' stupidity. Who did they think they'd fool? No one who had any experience with codes, certainly, and no one with any time. He had lots of time, hours of the stuff, days, weeks. His job was to take those hours and spend them deciphering strings of numbers.

In under five minutes he had the message. *Shipment at five, Tuesday. Full load.* Everything else was just cover, dummy numbers, leads that went nowhere.

Of course, knowing that a shipment of something was coming in at five on Tuesday wasn't much of a lead either, but if whoever found the code knew who sent it, or to whom, and had a sense of their operation, it would probably be all they needed. He wrote the message out by hand—nothing on a computer anymore, because security had been breached too many times—made a copy of it, and walked it over to Interdiction; you couldn't even trust the runners. Besides, he wanted to deliver it himself.

In Interdiction the phones were ringing, people running around. He took off his parka because it was hot. Humid too; the humidifiers were going full blast, moist air gusting from the vents.

Bookman was by a table, studying a map of the docks, bald black head shining.

Here, Walpeter said, handing him the memo. Bookman took it and laid it aside. Walpeter bent to the map himself.

These go together? he asked, nudging the memo and the map.

Think so. Not sure. Used to be they used the old air base out by Encino. But that's got hot.

You thinking boats?

I'm thinking boats.

Bookman didn't say anything else and Walpeter began to hum some old blues licks, wandering away after a few moments with no response from Bookman. He'd been hoping for a lunch invitation, but Bookman had obviously been preoccupied. Walpeter was still shy about going to the Dinosaur by himself, all those curious black faces wondering what he was after. It was a cop bar, and strictly speaking he was not a cop, and a black cop bar, and there was nowhere inside he could hide his three hundred pounds of pasty white flesh; at least in Bookman he had a kind of passport. He could sit at one of the varnished booths without being stared at and read all the letters from the old bluesmen posted on the walls, and, if he was lucky and one of them was in town, he'd get to hear a soundcheck set while he ate. Pulled pork or baby back rib sandwiches, PBR on tap, slaw, beans, corn bread, the best corn bread in the city. He always had a double order, and what he didn't finish he'd bring home to toast for breakfast the next day. Just thinking about it, he could smell it browning in the toaster.

Bookman seemed indifferent to him; he rarely spoke. But he never told Walpeter to get lost, the way most people in his own department and all the other cops did, so Walpeter never asked him to lunch. It was better this way, having a chance that Bookman liked him. Why ask and possibly find out otherwise? Besides, he'd been the first—and so far only—person ever to ask Walpeter to lunch.

Sure, Walpeter had said, trying to sound nonchalant though

convinced his suddenly elevated pulse was giving him away. He made an effort slow down his breathing. He counted to five before asking, Where?

I was thinking the Dinosaur, Bookman had said. He snapped his glasses inside a leather case and slipped the case in his jacket pocket. Guy fat as you, you were born for the blues.

That conversation made Walpeter smile as he pushed back through a long series of double doors to his own department. Each time he came through a pair of doors the weather changed. Humid, dry, blistering heat, cold so sharp the walls seemed frosted. Hackers had got into the building program and reset all the thermostats. The first time it happened Walpeter had the brilliant idea of shutting off the building computer, then restarting it. Only programs loaded onto the hard drive had been saved, and, when they'd done it and it had worked, Walpeter earned a brief celebrity. But four days later, after people had taken home their parkas and space heaters and fans to make room in their crowded offices, the hackers struck again, and this time their program was a worm that ate into other programs. Restarting the computer wouldn't kill it off. He couldn't use the office computers to break the code—the hackers' program contained a no-override provision—and it was taking a long time on his PC. It was unnetworked and hence untouchable but also small and slow; it had been two months now, and the questions from his coworkers about when he was going to break it were turning bitter.

He wasn't sure himself; the virus seemed also to have a self-mutating instruct that kept him off balance. He'd been close to cracking it the week before, but when he'd gone back into the code to check a certain sequence of numbers, the sequence was altered. His only hope was that the self-mutations had to be within a fairly narrow band, or else risk the entire program becoming unfocused. If he could swab the band, create the proper algorithm, he'd be all right. But that was a week or two away.

•

Why I like the blues. He put the pad to his chest and checked to be sure no one was coming; he could just imagine the crap he'd take, the practical jokes on line, in his office and his car, if anyone found him writing this. But there was no one; the linoleum floors glowed dully, the air conditioning was on, the windows were all fogged up. He wrote some more.

Think of the heroic Robert Johnson. Dying for the blues at twenty-seven. And Ditney Roberts, Bip Underwood, The Skipper. They'd seemed larger than life, he'd read books about them, there was even a movie about Johnson. No one was going to write about him, ever, but they weren't that far apart. Johnson said that the music was all in his head, he just wrote it down to get it out. Then new notes would fill up the space; he'd had no choice, the sound of them was driving him crazy. Walpeter felt the same about numbers. Strings of them, loops, endless equations. Hence codes; his mind worked in the language of computers, always had. When he was a boy his mother would pester him to go outside and play with the other neighborhood kids, and then find him half an hour later scratching a series of numbers into the hard Texas dirt with a stick. If she took that away he used pebbles as markers and went on. Sometimes he thought if you could cut a computer in half and he held one half in either hand, when you plugged the computer back in you wouldn't notice any difference, it would just be the numbers streaming through both halves and him. He didn't have any choice.

Why do you like the blues? Bookman said.

What? Walpeter slapped the pad to his chest so quickly the rush of air made his hair flip.

The blues. Bookman gestured at the pad.

Oh. I don't. Not really.

Really? Bookman started to turn away. I was going to see if you wanted to head to the Dinosaur. Skipper's in town. Warm-up set.

Wait! Walpeter stood so fast his chair fell over.

Bookman's eyebrows went up. He didn't have to say what he was thinking.

No, I'm all right. Just distracted.

And the blues?

I do like them, but this was work.

You've lost me.

Well. Walpeter felt himself blushing, the red rising to his red hair like rosé filling a wineglass. I mean, the blues, yes, I like them. A lot. But this, he held up the pad, it's what I do to clear my mind out.

Oh, okay. Well, if the real thing'll clear your mind out some more, let's go.

Sure, thanks. Walpeter felt absurdly grateful, as if someone had let him into a club he'd waited forever to join. His third invitation in two weeks. He knew better than to say so; this club had rules, some of which you had to intuit: excessive gratitude was against them. Still, there had to be something he could do. As he got to the door and took off his parka it came to him.

Where's he playing tonight? he asked. The Skipper.

Bookman looked at him. The Dinosaur.

Oh, right. Walpeter felt his blush deepen, but he pushed on. Maybe I could grab a couple of tickets and we could go.

No tickets, Bookman said, and put on his fedora. Just donations. And the food bill. He started across the street and Walpeter felt the wind leaving his sails. Botched invitations weren't any better than no invitation at all.

Bookman reached the far curb and turned back. But we can go if you want. Should be good. Let's hurry now, though, so we'll have something to compare it to.

•

In the bar Walpeter leaned over the table, menu crumpling against his chest.

So, did you figure it out? Where on the docks?

Bookman looked up from his menu. He'd been studying it as if it were in code. He waved one finger back and forth and said, The pulled pork for me today, Carolina style. I could use a little vinegar. You?

Same, Walpeter said. With an extra order of green beans.

Good, got to keep yourself in shape, Bookman said and smiled. Keep everything regular.

They ate, listened to the music; Walpeter felt himself vaguely dissatisfied. On the way out, Bookman sighed. Curtis Maytone had been disappointing, lots of scales on his guitar, a few signature licks, but mostly he'd spent the time making up nonsense lyrics to go along with other people's music. They felt the same thing!

Bookman put his hat on and adjusted the brim. Not quite rakish, Walpeter thought, but definitely individualized. He could learn a lot from Bookman. He was so excited his chest hurt. He wasn't very good at this friend thing.

I have a friend.

I have a friend.

Yes you do.

One one two, one one two, call and response; it was the blues. He wanted to hum it, he wanted to sing it, he wanted to shout it loud and proud as they wove through traffic back toward the station. But he didn't. Sirens were sounding up the street. Bookman glanced over his shoulder, pushed farther out into traffic. Back there, in the Dinosaur? he said, low enough that only Walpeter could hear. Don't ever talk about something I'm working on in public again.

Walpeter felt as if he'd been struck in the chest with a brick. Sorry, I didn't think. His throat closed up and he had to clear it to speak. It's a cop bar, he said, trying to explain himself.

Yep. That's exactly why.

Walpeter's chest hurt more. Since he was born for the blues, he knew what the next verse would be and how this would end, no matter how many times they went to lunch, even if they became closer than twins, even if he helped Bookman solve every case that ever came his way. Like everyone else you had a void and like everyone else you tried unsuccessfully to fill it; all you could do was sing it out.

I had a friend.
I had a friend.
Yes you did.

A Sharp Winter, an Obese Smile

All day my son was out and all day I fed my anger red meat: he wasn't respectful, he didn't do what I asked, he never thought about others. The trash, for instance: it hadn't been taken out, which meant I had to push the heavy wheeled bin up the long rutted driveway, weak arms and bad back and all.

My anger grew bigger and bigger, all chest and balls and sulfurous cologne; by the end of the day it was as big as the room. And still I fed it. I knew it would be explosive by the time he came home, and I didn't want that, so I carried it upstairs and stuffed it in my bedside table, one mottled foot refusing to be tucked away.

After midnight the door opened downstairs. He called up hello but didn't come up to see me, to tell me where he'd been. I heard him banging around in the kitchen, probably eating everything I'd ever bought, not caring that his noise was keeping me up, and running water for so long, I swore he was part camel.

Inside the drawer I heard my anger laughing. I opened the drawer and poked the anger with a pin. Oh, it didn't like that, was surprised and, of course, angry—the air left it with a miserable hiss of whispered imprecations *You never!*—but even deflated it was still there, recognizable, and I swallowed it.

I slept, though badly, my stomach in turmoil. Anger will have its way.

In the morning, I went by my son's darkened room, where he lay stretched out on his bed on his back, arms flung out to his sides as if crucified, snoring, his hairy legs exposed. It's I who's crucified, I said, looking at the clothes I'd washed strewn around the room, on the bed, the chair, the floor. On his lamp a purple shirt. Beside me, my anger flared again, the tiny chest ballooning, the swelling balls burning red, my daily companion, more regular than the newspaper and filled with similar vitriol. I told it to be quiet.

Downstairs, in the childishly pure morning light, I found the dishes done and put away, the serving spoons shining silver in their bins, the glasses gleaming on their ordered shelves. I hadn't even asked him to wash them! I leaned my head against the polished cool of the crumbless counter in gratitude and felt pride swelling beside me, all smooth face and supple hands, smelling of vanilla. I thought to check it—pride's as bad as bragging, after all—then let it go. Before long, its brother would have reason to expand again. Why not let that beautiful face have its hour?

On Board the SS Irresponsible

Bumping cautiously up the dirt driveway toward Clare's house, dust swirling behind him into the blue air, Buddy knew what Clare would say as soon as he got out of the car.

You're late, *Buddy*, fifty minutes late. She would say his name like that, italicized, as if having to pronounce it might give her a yeast infection, and then she'd go on. You said 9:45. Don't try to add this time onto the end of the visit.

And if she was really angry, she'd accuse him of going too fast on the driveway and stirring up the dust on purpose. His foot itched on the gas pedal, but he ignored it.

They were all waiting for him on the porch, and when he got to within twenty yards of the house the kids came boiling down the stairs, or the boys did, their blond hair bobbing in the sunlight; Bernice, always sensitive to her mother's feelings, held back. Buddy barely had the door open before the boys were jumping and pawing at him like puppies, the two of them yelling about what they wanted to do first: Simpler's Market to buy gum, the sporting goods store for new baseball gloves, the Gazebo for lunch and ice cream; he'd promised.

Now hold on, guys, he said, wrapping them both up and spinning around on the grass. They were heavy, they had their heads thrown back and their eyes closed and their mouths open, they were clutching at his clothes. He spun faster and faster and tucked his head between theirs; their hair smelled of shampoo and their small white teeth shone as they giggled. At last he slowed and released them and they wobbled and tumbled over one another, still giggling, and he stooped and put his hands on his knees to overcome his dizziness. The boys watched him from a tangle on the ground.

Daddy's got the day planned, he said.

The heat was damp and clinging; by the afternoon it would be murderous. The cicadas sounded like machinery. He pulled his shirt away from his chest as he stood and walked to the bottom of the stairs. Give your mother a kiss and then get in the car, and I'll tell you what's up while we're driving, he said. He certainly wasn't going to tell them in front of Clare.

Finally he looked at Clare, who was squinting and holding an apron to her face until the dust had settled; a long plume of it was still drifting by the house. She was in her Grandma Moses mode, Buddy thought—an old flower-print house dress and black lace-up ankle boots. It didn't surprise Buddy but it continued to puzzle him; for a woman who made so much money at work, she dressed like a pauper. She'd told him that was his problem: the things he worried about didn't matter, and the things that did he couldn't be bothered with.

Satisfied the air was fit to breathe again, Clare snapped out the apron and rested one arm across Bernice's bony shoulders.

You're late, *Buddy*, she said. Don't try to add this time onto the end of the visit.

Buddy sucked his teeth and stared at the field of oats across the driveway—blue-green and still in the wavering heat—and tried not to smile. No sense angering Clare by laughing: next time, she might not let them go at all. Divorce had taught him the value of ordering his desires in a way that marriage never had.

In the field a swallow swooped low and folded its wings and dropped onto an oat stalk, the stalk bobbing under the bird's weight and then springing back up again, and a yellow moth fluttered uncertainly across the long serrated rows of grain. The two contrary motions looked like some kind of child's game, and watching them brought on more dizziness. He turned back to the porch and cleared his throat.

I won't, Clare. Seven o'clock, right?

Six-thirty, she said. Too many drunks out driving on Saturday nights; I want them home well before dark. I know, Buddy. I work in hospital administration. I see the reports.

As if I didn't know, he thought. It was only after she'd gone to work at the hospital that things had turned sour, Clare suddenly ambitious in a way she'd never been before, bringing home reports to read and mark up every night, spending hours in front of her computer researching other hospitals' websites, urging him to go back to school and make something of himself too.

I'm already something, he'd finally told her after months of sloughing it off. He was in the kitchen, leaning against the counter, and outside in the indigo sky the first stars glowed, silver and green. It was something that in the past she would have remarked upon. He put his coffee cup in the sink and faced her and said, I'm a landscaper.

You're not a landscaper. You cut people's lawns.

I'm a landscaper, and I know things.

You know things?

I know things. There's four types of soil. I'll bet you didn't know that. Or why sumacs are the first trees to grow on swampy ground.

Those are facts, Buddy, not knowledge. You're always confusing the two. Then she left the room and that was that.

At last Clare gave Bernice's shoulders a squeeze, releasing her, and she skipped down the stairs to greet Buddy, offering her cheek for a kiss.

He gave her a brief hug and said, You ready for a good day?

I sure am, Daddy.

Good girl, he said, and hugged her harder. Her bones felt as delicate as a bird's.

After Bernice climbed into the car, he said, Six-thirty's fine by me.

The boys kissed their mother and sprung off the porch; the car rocked under their tumbling weight.

I've got a lot planned, Buddy said to Clare. He shut the door and walked around the car. But I don't have a number you can reach us at.

Clare moved to the edge of the porch, shaking her head and holding up both hands, palms out. Oh no, Buddy, she said. That's quite all right. Don't tell me more. I'm always better off not knowing what your plans are.

Well. He tossed the keys and caught them. Love to stay and chat, but the meter's ticking.

Without waving, he climbed in and drove off, faster than he had to, kicking up pebbles against the undercarriage and a cloud of dust behind the car. In no time, the cloud had obscured his view of Clare, who was standing by one of the white pillars in her limp yellow dress with the apron up over her face again, watching them, and when they turned onto the road and he looked back, she was gone.

They were going fishing at a favorite spot of Buddy's from long ago. Fields of wild grass surrounded the stream, hills the kids could roll down, a forest of glinting birch and somber pine. There were train tracks too, and if a train went by they'd lay nickels on the rails for the wheels to flatten; he'd brought along a dozen.

Bernice was happy, but the boys sounded disappointed.

There'll be something there you like, Buddy said. I guarantee it.

What? Zach said. Of the three, he was the quickest to suspicion, often announcing that he didn't like new things—shoes, cereal, amusement park rides—and refusing to try them until after a long battle, a battle which Buddy hoped to forestall.

If I tell you, it won't be a surprise.

I don't like surprises.

You will this one.

Zach frowned, and Buddy decided to try another tack, asking about school and friends and the farm.

How's Mom doing, he said. Not yelling too much?

Don't even try, Dad, Bernice said, looking up from her book, a history of dinosaurs he'd given her once they reached the highway. And don't *you* answer either, she said to her brothers. He just wants to know so he can start a fight with Mom, and if that happens, *we're* the ones who'll get in trouble.

I don't want to fight with Mom, Bernice. I just want to know how you're doing.

We're doing fine, Dad. And we're with you. She smiled at him in the mirror and moved aside a strand of hair which had blown over her eyes, and the habitual gesture pleased him: he missed most the contrarian minutiae of the family's daily life, routines for breakfast and bed, long-standing arguments about chores, the sound of children breathing in the night. Who would have guessed? Without it, most nights he slept poorly.

Still, he was glad Bernice had told him to stop poking around the edges of their life; Clare could be bossy, yet Bernice wasn't going to have any trouble standing up to her, or to him. Good for her.

A few minutes later they turned off the highway to a county road, which smelled of freshly mown hay, and after two miles they came upon a woman out running. Twenty, Buddy guessed, maybe twenty-two, a leggy redhead. He'd always had a thing for red hair. At one point, early on, Clare had dyed her hair to please him, but then later, after the fights began, she'd told him his pleasure in it was just one more sign of his immaturity.

That had seemed doubly unfair, bringing up the past in order to wound him, and in doing so transforming a pleasant memory into a weapon, and he realized now that right then he should have seen it: if their shared past was becoming treacherous, the future could only be worse.

He slowed because they were going to pass the runner near a turn and he didn't want to crowd her if a car swung wide coming in the other direction; she'd have only the rock-lined drainage ditch to jump into. She wore a black jogging bra and fluorescent green shorts. As the distance shrank between her and the hood of the car, Ted started talking about school. He was learning math.

One times ten is ten, he said.

That's right, Buddy said. Good for you. You really are learning it.

They were in the curve now, no other cars coming. Buddy gave the woman plenty of room and then she was behind him. In the rearview he couldn't see much of her, just her shoulders and the bobbing hair, but in the side-view mirror he could make out the smooth skin of her thighs, shiny with sweat and a summer tan, and the black bra. A small silver necklace bounced as she ran, flashing in the sun.

And two times ten is ten. And three times ten is ten.

Um-hmm.

Dad. Bernice slapped her book closed. Pay attention.

He flushed and caught her eye in the mirror. I am.

To the road, she said.

When he looked ahead, he was startled to see that he'd drifted into the other lane.

This is the surprise? Zach said. A boat? He kicked at the white gravel beside the aluminum fisher, the clicking sound of stone on stone briefly drowning out the hum of cicadas.

Not just any boat, a fishing boat, Bernice said. She ran her fingers along the polished gunwale. Cool, she said.

No it's not, Zach said. It's a boat.

But it's not the surprise, Buddy said. This is. He produced some cardboard cut-outs and three palm-sized cans of spray paint.

We're going to paint the boat? Ted said.

Great, Zach said, sitting on a log. We get to work all day.

Not the boat, Buddy said. Just its name. I want you guys to help me paint its name on.

He unfolded the stencils, which he'd made that morning, on one of the boat seats. Readying the stencils and driving the boat here were the reasons he'd been late. Unhitching the trailer took surprisingly long, but he'd kept at it, even while knowing his tardiness would inspire a tongue-lashing from Clare, because he wanted the day's events to be a surprise; showing up with the trailer would have ruined that. The children had had enough bad surprises recently, and he wanted to give them a good one to balance things out.

Bernice bent to read the stencils.

The S-S-Irr-e-spon-sible. Dad! she said, twirling to face him, her voice disapproving. But he could see she was trying not to smile. You can't name a boat that!

Come on, he said, and nudged her. Even your mother would have to laugh at that; it's what she always calls me.

But she wouldn't laugh, he knew that. She'd be galled that he'd made a joke of it, which was of course the larger part of the pleasure he took in it.

As Buddy shook the paint cans upside down, rattling the marbles inside, he told the boys they could each paint an S; Bernice would get to do the Irresponsible.

That's not fair, Ted said. She gets a lot more letters than we do.

He's right, Bernice said. Let's count them up and split them.

In the end they each got five. It made a mess; their hands were unsteady holding the stencils, the paint ran, and Zach didn't like it when Ted painted some of his R while doing his own.

Do his over, and then do yours, Buddy said.

No, Zach said. It won't work. He'll still have more. He already did his, and some of mine.

Do mine, then, Bernice said. I don't care.

Zach took both of their suggestions on his next turn, painting his brother's letters, his own, and some of Bernice's.

When they were done, they still had most of their cans left, though Buddy'd bought the smallest size.

Can we use these? Zach said, squatting by the creek. He watched a cricket hop from the shore to a damp gray rock in the water and then sprayed it with the paint.

Hey! Stop that! Buddy said, grabbing the can from him. The cricket tried to spread its painted wings, then toppled into the water and spun away, legs working frantically.

Da-ad, it's fun, Zach said.

Bernice sprayed her can into the air. The blue mist smelled like banana oil and drifted down like fireworks.

He could see her point. Why have paint cans if they couldn't use them? He handed the can back to Zach. All right, he said. But one place only, those timbers. He pointed out the railroad bridge under which the creek flowed, narrowing like the waist of an hourglass.

There's lots of nasty words on them you can cover up. Anywhere else would just be making a mess.

But I can't read! Ted and Zach said in unison.

Bernice can, Buddy said.

As they were walking off, he said, Nothing else, understand? Don't paint the grass. I don't want something I have to clean up. He stood back to inspect the boat.

•

Each of them ended up with one blue hand, but Buddy counted the painting a success, as did the children. He'd known they would, just as he'd known that if he told Clare she'd have called him a fool. A waste of time, she would have said.

But it wasn't. Painting the silly name on the boat, along with the heat, the song of the crickets and the smell of the pungent grass—these were things they'd remember for the rest of their lives. As a teenager, he'd swum here often, cooling off in the deep pools after days spent working on neighboring farms or for his uncle's landscaping business, and he'd planned this day after recalling his own. Still ahead were a picnic, and fishing from the boat, and sugar cubes and carrots to feed a swayback horse that sometimes wandered down from the surrounding fields for a drink; the memories they'd take away would be great ones. Blue hands. Who could ever forget that?

Hey guys, he said. They were upending rocks and shouting out their finds, salamanders and crayfish, a colony of potato bugs. He said, Let's take the boat out on its inaugural cruise.

They sprinted back along the shore, Ted splashing through the water, and when they got to the boat Buddy handed out lifejackets.

Do we have to? Zach said, dropping the bulky orange bib to the grass. I'm hot, Daddy, and they make me look goofy.

That's why you have a dad, Buddy said. To embarrass you. Go on now, put it on. I'll show you how we're going to cool off.

Once they were all in the boat he pushed off, the bottom scraping over the gravel, and jumped aboard himself, the gunwale rocking to within inches of the water from his weight. Bernice giggled at the motion, but Zach's face paled; he looked as though he might get sick.

What's the matter, Zach? Buddy said, rocking the boat again as he sat. I thought you liked rides.

I do, he said. But I've never been on a boat before.

Use the oars, Dad, Bernice said. Make us go fast.

Oars? He shifted his legs and looked beneath them. No oars on this trip.

But how will we go?

The boat was drifting over the brilliant water, spinning, the bow turning from east to west in the slow current.

First time a boat hits the water it's not supposed to go, Buddy said.

What? Zach said. It's supposed to sink?

No. Flip. Like this.

Buddy grabbed the gunwales and began throwing his weight rapidly back and forth, trying to flip it. Come on, he said. Help me.

After a surprised few seconds, when they weren't quite sure he meant it, all three children started moving too, out of sync at first, and the boat rocked less than it had initially, but after a few tries they got the boat to truly sway. Up went one side, the far gunwale touched the water, everything hung in the balance, and then giggling they shifted their weight and the boat tilted back and slapped down on the water and splashed them and began to tip up the other way.

At last they overbalanced, and with the boys screaming with delight and Buddy bellowing and Bernice wide-eyed and oddly silent, the boat flipped over on top of them, and when Buddy surfaced, laughing, Bernice was standing in knee deep water, shouting. He mistook the sound for laughter and tried to hug her, to share her joy, but she slapped his hand away and screamed even louder.

Daddy! That hurt! Now he could see she was crying. You could have hurt the boys! she said. The boys were fine, kneeling a bit stunned in the shallows, looking from him and Bernice to the overturned boat, but he was sure that if Bernice hadn't been angry, they'd be laughing too.

Bernice, he said. Come on. We needed to cool off, and it was a joke. No one was going to get hurt. I left the oars out on purpose, and why do you think I had you wear the lifejackets?

I got hurt, Daddy. My *head*. She placed her palm flat on top of it. The boat hit me when we flipped over, and I stubbed my wrist on a stone.

You stubbed your wrist? he said, thinking a joke might still turn her anger around. At least you didn't sprain your nose.

Daddy. She tried to stomp her foot but succeeded only in splashing herself. You *know* what I mean.

He leaned on the overturned hull, his shoulders sagging. I'm sorry, he said, torn between wanting to tell her to lighten up and genuinely feeling foolish. Can you forgive me?

I will, Ted said.

Me too, said Zach. He was squeezing water from his hair. Let's do it again.

No, Bernice said. And Mummy won't forgive you, either. You're the adult. You're supposed to know better. When she pulled her hand from her head, blood spotted the palm. See, she said, holding it up to show him. I told you it was a stupid thing to do.

Oh Sweetie, he said, slogging through the water toward her. Let me help you.

No thank you, she said, unsnapping the lifejacket and flinging it to the muddy shore. You've helped enough.

When she was out of the water, she twisted water from her shorts and began to walk. She said, If we weren't so far away, I'd walk home and leave you three fools alone.

God, Ted said. We should change her name to Mom, Junior.

He gave them Cracker Jacks and let them explore on their own. Bernice would come around, she always did. It was simply a matter of waiting until she brought him some trophy she discovered, a fossilized bug or leaf, a stone with a vein of mica. Her cut had been nothing, no more than a scratch, really, but righting the boat was harder work than he'd expected; he had to hold it steady in the current and the water trapped beneath the seats was enormously heavy, and he had to lift the boat a few inches at a time and let the water drain out without setting it down for a rest. If he did, all the water flowed back in.

Done, he beached the boat and sat on it to catch his breath. His wet clothes smelled swampy. He'd have to shower the kids before bringing them back, but that would be all right; they liked his apartment, and he could throw their clothes in the washer and dryer while they bathed, let them eat popcorn and watch a movie.

He lay down on the warm gravel to dry himself after sifting out the sharpest pieces, and it was surprisingly comfortable, but the sun was blinding. Still, he decided against switching to the shady side of the boat—if he did, his clothes wouldn't dry—and he pulled the brim of his hat over his eyes instead. He could hear the children, talking, laughing, moving away toward the railroad bridge, Bernice's voice the loudest. Perhaps he should be worried, but they were miles from nowhere; what could happen to them? The water at its deepest rose only to the boys' waists and Bernice's hips, and they all knew how to swim. He settled back and listened to Bernice tell the boys what to look for, the rounded stones she wanted, and then a little later, after a silence, he heard her say her head felt fine, really she'd just been scared, and she shouldn't have yelled at Daddy like that.

Like what? Zach said. His voice was a little higher and even from a distance Buddy could always distinguish it from his brother's, which gladdened him, and then Bernice was screaming. Buddy shifted on the gravel, waiting for her demonstration to stop, and when it didn't her screams began to sound ominous. He sat up sweating and realized from the sun's position, directly overhead now, that he'd drifted off, and then he heard two of them screaming at least, and he stood and started running.

What is it? he yelled. Tell me who's hurt!

He thought it must be that a snake had bitten them, and he tried to remember if he'd ever seen rattlers or copperheads nearby, or even heard of them being in the area. One leg was asleep and he couldn't move fast enough on the slippery rocks, and he hoped they weren't near the water. Why hadn't he made them keep their lifejackets on? Clare would cut off his balls.

But no one was hurt. The three of them were running down a hill on the other side of the bridge through the long green grass toward the water, stopping at its edge, screaming, giggling, playing tag, their faces bright red with joy. When his breathing calmed down, when his anger did, his nerves, Buddy joined the game. A trio of white butterflies, startled by their passage, floated up behind them.

Next came the picnic. Buddy persuaded them to rejoin him in the boat, after swearing solemnly and repeatedly that he wouldn't tip it over again, and they pushed off with the picnic basket on the middle seat between them. When they were far enough out in the creek to escape the mosquitoes, he dropped the steel anchor and waited for the boat to swing round before handing out the food. Smoked ham and Genoa salami for everybody, pastrami and artichoke hearts for Ted, fresh rolls and bags of chips and cooled bottles of lemonade. It was a grand success.

What about you, Daddy? Zach asked, after Buddy had served them all. What are you going to drink?

No more lemonade in the cooler? he asked.

Bernice checked. Three bottles, Daddy. She tried to hand him one.

Buddy waved her off and said, Those are yours, I'm afraid.

No, Daddy. Have one.

Absolutely not. I brought two for each of you, and two you'll have. He picked up a fishing rod that had been lying beside him, the line out and disappearing into the water, and began to reel it in. He said, Let's see what the river gods have left us.

The pole bent immediately, as under a great weight. All three children stopped eating to watch. Ah, he said, reaching into the cool water to grasp something. They've been kind, he said. He pulled up a quart bottle of root beer, water coursing down its brown smooth glass. Enough for me and for you, Buddy said.

Dad, Bernice said. Mom's against that.

Against what? Zach said.

You mean other than the entire twentieth century? Buddy said.

Dad!

It always amazed him how she could italicize her words just like her mother.

I'm kidding, Bernice, and I'm not going to let you drink this. I know Mom doesn't give you soda. It's to christen the boat.

But he hadn't been kidding. After getting her degree in Health Administration and starting to work at the hospital, Clare had been transformed into one of her grim Scottish ancestors, working ridiculous hours and banning television and radio from the house. The funbuster, he'd taken to calling her. She kept her computer—she needed it for work—but everything else that smacked of modernity had to go. Evidently sex had been part of that package, and then he himself was.

He sluiced the water from the bottle with his hand and gripped it by the neck.

Ready? he said.

They nodded.

Head averted, he clinked it gently against the bow, and then again, harder, when it didn't break. After a third time, he sighed and brought the bottle back on board.

Let me try, Zach said, scrambling over the seat toward him, one hand held out for the bottle.

No. Buddy put his hand on Zach's shoulder and gently pushed him down. It might break in your hand and cut you, he said.

He studied the bottle. A small plane passed high overhead, its engine note as faint as an insect's call. Speaking of cuts, he said, it's probably not a good idea to break this and have glass lying around. People wade in this stream, fishermen. I guess we'll have to drink it after all.

Bernice scowled and shook her head but didn't say anything, so Buddy waited until she was busy eating her lunch before unscrewing the cap and starting to drink, and when she wasn't looking, he poured some into the boys' empty lemonade bottles.

After dessert—cupcakes, fresh from the Sweetheart Bakery— they began to fish. They weren't catching anything, but that was all right; mostly it was time for teasing and telling jokes. They finished the root beer, the heat settled, a white rim appeared at the edges of the sky. Eventually, after half an hour or so, the children grew silent, and then, one by one, they laid down their rods and climbed out of the boat and waded to shore, with Bernice being the last to go. Buddy decided to keep fishing, wanting to catch something for dinner, a sunfish, a trout, whatever might be around, but he knew it was time to let them go. Stay close, he called out to them. And stay close together. This time he made them keep on their lifejackets.

From the heat and the lack of sleep he began to lose himself in reverie as the boat eddied in the current, remembering—

though he tried not to—coming here with Clare on their first date, and how he'd chosen the spot because the night was steaming and the water would be hard to resist. There was a full moon. She'd been wearing too much perfume, something flowery, and he'd loved it. They'd talked, laughed, walked over the tarry railroad bridge holding hands, and to impress her he'd climbed out onto where the ties extended into space and hopped from one to another, eyes closed, arms held out for balance, and then maneuvered her into betting him he wouldn't jump into the water below, swollen by summer storms, and finally said he'd do it only if she did too. He'd leaped and she'd followed right after. When she climbed out, her soaked blouse had clung to her breasts and water dripped from her hair down her glistening throat. At the thought of it, he felt himself stiffening with desire, which made him remember other trips here with Clare, how during the following months they made love on the hot dusty rocks under the railroad bridge with the train pounding by overhead, the way the struts creaked and shivered, the shifting of the timbers. His memory was so vivid he heard the whistle of an approaching train.

Then the whistle sounded again, puzzling him, until he realized it was a real train, heading their way.

Hear that, kids? he said, setting down the fishing pole. Time to put the nickels on the tracks. He reached into his damp front pocket for them.

The children didn't respond, and the whistle blew again and then again right after. The train was making noise now too, getting closer, an electric humming and the wheels clicking over spacers and some kind of odd, mechanical squealing that sounded like brakes, and it caused him to turn his head up toward the tracks. The children were on the trestle, running, their orange lifejackets like kites in front of them, pulling them on but slowing them up, and the train was rounding the bend on the berm, bearing down on them. He felt the water move beneath him from the train shaking the ground, and the train was so big it looked impossibly close. The whistle now wasn't stopping.

He was in the water and then he was on the shore. Jump, he screamed, good God run, and he was running too, sodden feet slipping on the shale, moving in the same direction the children were, screaming over and over for them to jump. The water was deep enough they had their lifejackets they'd be fine if only they jumped. They didn't jump, they seemed not to hear him. They were running straight ahead, they had thirty-five yards to go to the end of the bridge, thirty maybe, the train a quarter-mile. In the heat waves rising from the steel tracks, they shimmered as they ran, as if they were ghosts.

The whistle wouldn't stop and he wouldn't take his eyes off them, not allowing the train into his field of vision as if that might protect them, and then he was doing calculations: they were going to make it, they weren't going to make it, they were going to make it with seconds to spare. Finally, he had no choice, he had to look at the train. Sparks and smoke were coming from the wheels, he hadn't known steel could do that, and the engineer was leaning so far out the window that he seemed in danger of falling, waving something blue. His mouth was open wider than a cave and he must have been screaming too, but Buddy couldn't hear him over the noise of the squealing wheels; the train had reached the bridge. The first timbers shivered from the weight and then he watched the shiver move down the timbers in front of the train like a wave, and then he looked back at his children, and he knew, knew in a way that turned his bones liquid, dropping him to his knees on the sharp stones where he began to cry, knew they were going to make it.

Ten yards, he guessed, two or three seconds they'd have after they leaped to safety and the oncoming train obliterated the space they'd just vacated, passing close enough to slice through their shadows but far, far away from touching their corporeal bodies. The tears, the hugging, the terrified children, the admission to Clare and her blistering response, everything that would transpire from this moment on, he saw it all, knew what it was going to be like, and for the punishments that he would have to endure, he was grateful.

Hours later, when he pulled into the driveway to Clare's house, his house—he reminded himself, he'd never insisted she pay him for his half though he could have—a few lights were on. He stopped fifty yards away and cut his headlights and worked through them. The kitchen, the front hallway, Bernice's room upstairs. That one he looked at the longest. He knew them all, the yellow squares against the dark, but what good did knowing do? He'd known the house was his when he signed the papers on it with Clare, known that he and Clare would grow old there, watching their kids grow up and play in the surrounding fields, had even known how the three of them would look bundled up in their snowsuits as they rolled down the snowy woodpile on the coldest, clearest days of winter, while he watched from behind the window by the sink, a cup of steaming coffee in his hand. But he'd never seen anything like that. In June they'd moved in, and by August Clare had asked for a divorce, and when he'd suggested counseling, she told him to get as much as he wanted. Knowing something didn't make it true.

He got back in and gunned the engine, loud enough for Clare to hear, and turned on the lights. She'd know some things too. That it was his car coming up the drive, that he was hours late, that her ex-husband was a fool and that she was a lucky woman to be rid of him. But there were other things she wouldn't know.

She wouldn't know that at the last instant one of the boys

had stumbled and fallen, Ted, he thought, though he'd never be sure, and that the other two had kept going and made it to safety, Bernice in the lead, her usual spot, her brother only a step behind. Or that he'd found himself still screaming even though he knew she couldn't hear him over the approaching roar of the train and the train's shrill whistle and the fear and blood which must have been thundering in her own head as it was in his, screaming because he knew she could read his lips, Jump please jump for God's sake jump, just for even one of his kids to live, that's all he wanted, don't do the right thing, he was begging her even as he knew she wouldn't listen because she'd always been Clare's daughter and not his, or that she leaned over the edge and peered down at him for no more than a second, watching his lips move, her face pale and round over the orange bib of the lifejacket, or that she'd straightened then and turned away, back toward her brother, back toward the oncoming train, pulling her other brother by the hand.

Or that even then, once they'd grabbed their other brother, it had seemed they might still have a chance, and that his heart had lifted to see the three of them up and running again for the end of the bridge, running, running, running, their hair streaming and their legs pumping and their mouths open, until he had realized it was far too slowly and much too late, or that the train had caught them, all of them, as one, in a single, sickeningly swift instant.

Or that when the police had come, and the firemen, and later the cameraman from a local news station, that he had told them all that the children's mother was dead, because it was news she should get not from a stranger, but from him, and that along with the officials he'd spent a horrifying and fruitless two hours searching for a last, blue hand.

No, she wouldn't know any of that. He wanted her to hold on to her ignorance and to her anger, sure of her anger's righteousness as she rose from her chair and strode down the hallway and threw open the door and let light spill out over the porch to guide him in from the darkness, before other emotions took over that had nothing to do with him, because he knew now that knowing things was worthless, and that she was about to discover that what she'd known all along was true. He slowed up. For a few seconds more, he wanted to spare her that knowledge.

Immanent in the Last Sheaf

When the god came to them he was very sick. They found him face down near the rabbits and thought he was dead, but when they rolled him over he was still breathing: thin blue smoke when he exhaled, the quaking aspen leaves flickering silver and green as he inhaled and his old chest rose. His skin had yellowed and grown horny and he smelled sulfurous, but his eyes were normal, so he probably wasn't from the underworld, though they'd given up trying to determine the gods' origins. One they had thought was related to the wind was really water; they'd released flower petals from a hilltop on a blustery day and had a week of flooding rains until they'd rectified their mistake, so it was better not to guess than to guess incorrectly.

They put him in an upstairs room and fed and washed him, but he sickened and died. All night they lay awake because the god was lying dead in the next room. His silence was like a stone; it felt as if it might shift and crush them. In the morning she cut wood for the fire and he made bread. They ate in silence. Moss tea, apricot jam, a spoonful of precious honey.

After breakfast they disrobed the god and bathed him and anointed him with honey and carried him outside and let the ants devour him; his clothes too, which they'd buttered. Then they stood shoulder to shoulder waiting by the busy anthill, whose occupants would in the future come and swarm their feet but no longer into their house or barn, watching for the next god to breast the hills. They hoped for a woman. If she died too, they could appease the owls.

Find Your Real Job and Do It

I'm good with voices—we all are, it's why we're here—so it's driving me nuts that my best Latino doesn't get to the guy on the other end of the phone. Representative Gonzalez supports ending immigration quotas, I say, rolling my *r*'s. He wants to open the doors, like me, like joo.

I wait, let that hang. The guy's wife just lost her job for Christ's sake—oppo research turned up her unemployment claim—probably to an immigrant, and he ought to be biting.

I wait longer, listening to Otis beside me, whose accent is off—he's fine with the angry black man (which he is) and the lisping indeterminate male, but almost anything Hispanic gives him a bit of trouble—yet I like Otis's style. Who else would pay for his plane ticket to prison with a forged check? Oddly he does a fantastic Pacino. *Joo talking to me?* I always imagine the people on the other end panicking. *We fucked up this time, Martha. And he knows our number!*

I start to say something—though it's rare that anyone can wait me out—when the guy breathes deeply and coughs twice, a familiar tick, and I glance at the name again and realize I called him months before. John Q. Smith. I didn't get to him that time, either.

That's good, Smith says. About immigration. We should be a generous nation.

I look around, wondering which paint can he soaked his brain in. Forty phones, fluorescent lights, computers loaded with databases and the most basic spreadsheets (but no Internet connections), paper and pens. Most of us probably never saw this much stuff in one place in our lives except when we were ripping it off, and the government supplied none of it; *New Democracy* exists thanks to business.

But I agree, try pushing one or two other buttons for form's sake, and in the middle of the last one he says, Sorry, have to go. Wife's at the door with the groceries.

My in, I think, though I can't say how. I bluelight his name before moving on—a rare certain failure, but selective honesty keeps me here. Some of the others, they never figure that out: lie and they know you're lying, exile you to some shitty job in the laundry. Tompkins was the best I ever heard with voices, which only makes sense; he'd been an actor, if an out-of-work one for a long time before he burned down his apartment building. Arson, though he claims it was an accident.

Drunk and depressed he didn't get some part (*You don't look much like your head shot*), he came home to find himself locked out over three months back rent, tried sneaking in to an open window—not his—and dropped the bottle into the room, knocked over a candle, and, in his words, *Poof!*

But who knows? I've told a hundred different versions of my story; parts of all were true. Tompkins never copped to a single failed call and was gone after two weeks.

I move down my list, get the usual quota of lonely ones, especially older women, the kind Bimbo—in for milking them of their savings—gravitates to. He's got a photographic memory and I swear he's memorizing their names and numbers for when he gets out. Ten years; with luck most of them'll be dead.

Now and then just for fun I ask for social security numbers, surprised as always at how often people give them up. I'm careful, since they check our calls, but I can see Potts in the back, glancing up when he's about to flick the switch and listen. Through all of it Mr. J. Q. Smith keeps nagging at me; not this call, not my previous one months back—an unsuccessful attempt to siphon off Democratic support by convincing him to vote Green—but that wife of his.

It gets under my skin. I don't like losing—hate it—part of what I've learned in talk therapy (Rehab-blabathon) but it bugs me so much I'm off on most of my calls. I won't make the day's quota and Potts will ride me, but it's all right; I'm up for the week and a rare miss won't send me packing, though it's brutal here—miss quota three weeks in a row and you're toast.

Fifteen minutes before shutdown, I tweak Bimbo about his memory. We all like to test him, so he's not suspicious, but he gives the expected response: What do I get?

I pause as if I'm thinking—the power of the pause another thing I've learned in here—start punching in numbers as if I'm making a call. Fags, I say, knowing he'll turn me down.

He shakes his head, goes on with his call, when he's done and has redlined it on his computer, says, Got too many as it is.

He's not much of a smoker, which fact I knew. Two more calls and I say, Mags.

He shakes his head again, though they're good ones, *Penthouse*, sent by Belinda Marie. Her first six months of letters I never answered—she got my name from some church group prison directory—until she wrote once and said, Why don't you ever write back?

I don't believe in God. My entire letter, the first I ever sent without a lie.

I knew what she'd write back: *But He believes in you!* She surprised me. For a month I didn't hear from her. I was glad, wanting someone to be more stubborn than me, then disappointed when a package arrived from her address, no letter but three *Penthouse*s, as if she'd been saving them up. Now they arrive once a month and are worth a lot—I keep them near mint—but Bimbo's bent for older women and I'd known he wouldn't bite.

My heart rate picks up and I make myself breathe deeply. All right, I say with two minutes left, and snap my fingers as if I've just come up with it, Potts looking up at the sound. He goes back to his book and I think, *It's going to be like offering a smoothie to a kid.* Tomorrow's Wednesday, I say. My dinner.

Bimbo's beady eyes pop open and, though I've seen it a few times, the effect still startles me; it's as if someone's pushed two blue marbles through a wall of dough. A photographic memory but he can't recall I hate liver, so he thinks I'm sacrificing a lot and he's won; once you've said it you can't take it back. He can barely contain his smile.

Locked and loaded, he says.

Here. I one-eighty the list for him. This whole page.

Thirty seconds and he says, Done. A minute later Potts calls time.

In the morning I still haven't figured it out. The yard's steaming in the heat, like God's pissed on the world, and I don't throw a ball with the newbies or walk the walls with the short-timers, I stand and watch with the lifers; best time of the day to think. Like always, I imagine the drive home—I know the mileage cold, the route I'll take, estimate the time it'll take to within an hour—ending up in Harpersville just after dark. I'll pull up to the bookstore, shine the lights on the window, look in at all those titles.

I'll be able to afford a lot, even with my fifty-four-cents-an-hour salary. Buy them, read them, sell them again. But I won't donate any to a prison. *Screw the bastards. If they're dumb enough to get caught, they deserve everything they get.*

The memory makes me laugh, a line from one of our most successful drives, Cupcake Prisons, targeting Democrats who'd been recent victims of crime.

Outside the windows Borrows had gone by, pushing the book cart, and I thought, *Bingo*.

Let me ask you something, I said to one guy I called. You ever use the library?

Sure.

Thought so. Then let me ask you this. When was the last time the library delivered?

A laugh.

That's what they do here—I realized my slip—here in these prisons. Door-to-door service. The prisoners order the books they want, and the next day they're brought to their cells. True, but only after lockdowns, which fact doesn't matter to those listening; flip one tile and the rest come easily. We needed to sway a couple hundred votes and got over three thousand.

Now when weights break or the library floods, nothing gets replaced. Slitting our own throats, but none of us ever believes we're destined to stay here long. No violents among us; fraud, counterfeiting, the like. On the form all of us who can read check the same box: *Maladjusted, hoping to change.*

A group goes by, ready for work, Tompkins among them, Otis, Parker. Parker had been okay with voices but lost his spot over phone sex. We all just stopped, listening, and Potts looked up at the silence. Then Parker's booming basso cut through it. *Lady, when I'm done, you'll be able to drive a truck through it.*

Behind him is Pretty Boy. He had a face like a flounder to begin with, which wasn't improved by his wife. She found him cheating with her sister, took a hot iron to one side while he was sleeping; the thing none of us can figure out is how he's the one who ended up in here, but just the sight of him gives me an idea. I flick my cigarette away and join the line. That blue highlight of Smith is going to be lying in chalk.

•

Five minutes past Potts's first check, I say, Smith, John, and ignore Bimbo's droning response. Potts's eyes walk around the room again and I say, Smith, John A., and ignore Bimbo once more. Two phone calls later—about which I couldn't tell you a thing—I say, Smith, John Q., and punch in the numbers Bimbo repeats.

Eight-fifteen. She's fifty, probably embarrassed to be out of work for the first time, and I'm betting she's an early riser, pouring through the want ads with a red pen, hoping, and that Dear John is already at work and won't answer the phone.

Two for two; she picks up on the first ring. I clear my throat, launch into my Southern Belle. A bit rusty, but after the first stumbling words it flows.

Adrienne? I say. John's told me so much about you. At lunch, he couldn't talk about anything else.

I'm sorry? she says. Who is this?

I giggle, a nice touch, and Otis smiles conspiratorially; he'd been the first to try going female. Oh, I'm sorry, I say. Belinda Marie. Hasn't John told you about me? We've spent so much time working for Hector Gonzalez.

Gonzalez's Open Borders proposal, John's passionate advocacy, I go on until she begins asking questions, which soon turn random and disconnected, and I know I've tapped her, those first flutters of what I always feel myself, so I wrap up and sign off. Next on my list are ones I didn't get to yesterday, and if I'm going to make quota I have to hit hard. I pause for only a second. Truth is, it was like any other call: doubt and fear. Raise the first, incite the second.

Freeloading blacks, shifty Hispanics, an unfaithful husband? I'm just a voice in people's ears; anything I unlock inside them, it was already there. Don't blame me for being good at my job.

The Caricaturist's Daughter

Bernadette lay still in the blue light of morning, her face a shallow pool, resisting the ancient daily temptation to run her hand over her absent features. Coffee was brewing in the kitchen, so it wouldn't be long now; still, it was a pain to wait for her father to draw her face every morning before school, especially now that he was drinking again. But Bernadette had learned over time not to let her impatience show. If she did, he'd exaggerate her frowns, or make her head narrow and pointy with a wisp of smoke over it, and all day kids would make fun of her.

That had started early on. When she was four, she and her father were out for their nightly after-dinner walk, and Bernadette told her father she was going to run into the street.

No, you won't, he said. It's dangerous.

I'm going to, she said, standing on the soft green grass between street and sidewalk, tempted by the smooth gray ribbon unspooling before her that smelled of tar.

If you do, you'll regret it.

She touched her toe to the pavement and her father picked her up and carried her all the way home, ignoring her howls of sadness, her promises to never do it again, and in the morning she woke to the indignity of gigantic oversized clown feet, which made it impossible to run or ride her tricycle. In the end, she suffered through it for six months, even though she begged him every day to change them back.

And every day, he looked at her over the top of his glasses, pencil poised in his elegant left hand, and said, I want you to remember that lesson.

As she got older, she suspected he hadn't wanted to disappoint his readers, since they told him in long letters that they loved the little girl Bernadette with the big feet and her endless, stumbling misadventures; he would read to her from them now and then, and every year at the anniversary of her toe-in-the-street debacle she had to put up with the clown feet for twenty-four hours.

It came not to bother her, as she learned to get her schoolwork done ahead of time and would simply call in sick; she could do a great imitation of her mother's English accent (which was occasional and never pronounced) though she began to wonder why she couldn't draw, not even a straight line with a ruler. What use was mimicry?

At seven, she'd thought it might even be dangerous, after she heard her parents having sex—though at the time she didn't know that's what it was—and asked at breakfast if they were all right.

Her father said, Why?

I heard you both last night, she said, and I thought you were sick. Then she imitated each of them moaning to perfection.

Her mother turned bright red and her father said, You know, your ears are too big.

Dad! she said, at the same time her mother said, Hugh! but he didn't listen to either of them and drew her as Dumbo. We all have things to learn, he told her when she stood in the door, sobbing and not wanting to go to school, and you've got to learn when not to listen.

That lasted a week, until she fell and scraped her knees during a windstorm and her mother put her foot down and told her father he had to stop.

But it carried over into his work. In addition to his carica-

tures he drew two weekly comic strips—*The Barking Dog* and
It's About Time. In the first, a nice father had a feckless daughter
Belinda, who found her ears growing each time she walked the
dog (who barked endlessly and in every panel) and in the second, the girl Bernice was always late for school. In order to cure
that, her father gave her an oversized paper watch that weighed
down her arm.

At twelve, Bernadette got her first period, and she was irritable
and bloated and had terrible cramps. Her mother made her tea
with lots of sugar and kept her in bed with a hot water bottle,
and her father asked from out in the hallway, as if she might be
contagious, What's wrong?

She's like me, her mother said, pressing a cool washcloth to
Bernadette's forehead.

Her father, smoothing his tie, said, How?

When it's soup, her mother said, using her favorite
euphemism.

No kidding? her father said. God. The goddamn moon.
How did I ever get so lucky? Dragon-lady one and two, he said.
He shook his head and turned around and said, It would have
been easier if I'd had a son.

Which Bernadette thought was almost funny, because she'd
always thought it would have been easier if she'd had a sister,
or even a brother, someone else on whom her father could take
out his frustrations.

All afternoon the house was filled with the sound of his pencil scratching over the page and Bernadette's head began to hurt,
but she assumed it was just part of the peculiar things her body
was doing to her; she was horrified the next morning when she
awoke with grossly swollen feet covered in saddle shoes and enormous balloon-like hands in white gloves, but worst of all was
when she discovered her dragon head in the mirror.

That was a figure he returned to one week out of every four for a year, until she learned to keep her mood swings to herself, no matter how pronounced.

But now he'd started drinking, and some mornings it was nearly impossible to get him to draw much of anything. Day after day she went off as a smiley face, and she was getting tired of it; without a nose she couldn't tell if she had on too much perfume until people started making comments in the hallways, and on the morning of her French oral final he forgot her mouth altogether.

Even the letter he wrote, explaining it, didn't stop her from getting detention, and in response, he began drawing caricatures of Bernadette's French teacher in *It's About Time*.

Her real name was Madame Aimée Hinault, but in the strip he called her Mademoiselle Ample Hindquarters, drew her with a gigantic ass, and mangled her English, in small degrees. She had trouble with certain sounds, the voiced dental fricatives especially (just like her father) and yet Mademoiselle A. Hindquarters loved one book above all others and talked about it ceaselessly: *I Am Third*, by Gale Sayers. Of course, since she struggled with *Th*, whenever she spoke about the book she said, I am turd! which became her tagline, spoken at least once every day.

Madame Hinault was mortified, more by her newly giant rear end than by her problems with English, since her massive hindquarters were hard to cover up and trying to do so cost her a bundle in new clothes, but instead of being nice to Bernadette she grew meaner, and it seemed to drive her crazy that she couldn't get the smiley-faced Bernadette to frown. Eventually, Bernadette and her principal agreed she should switch to Spanish, where, it turned out, her teacher was worse: nearly deaf, he weighed over three hundred pounds and spent the morning dropping chips and popcorn on his sweatered belly, the afternoon plucking crumbs from the wool, her entire class period sleeping—but she was smart enough not to say anything to her father. She didn't want the whole school to turn against her.

The fan letters kept arriving, by the hundreds and then the thousands—her father had been voted the world's favorite cartoonist six years running (an honor he first campaigned for and now dreaded)—and he continued to read aloud from them, his gravelly baritone flooding with butterscotch as he repeated their praise, or turning bitter as old onions when those same fans asked what was next for Belinda and Bernice and Mademoiselle Ample Hindquarters.

Tomorrow and tomorrow and tomorrow, he shouted, the quotation gladdening her mother, despite his yelling (she had some English blood, she said, though she was never very precise about it). But those tomorrows did not make her father happy; the weight of them pouched his eyes and filled the pouches with liquid. The bourbon didn't help.

You don't help either, he said to her, when Bernadette pointed that out to him.

Me? What do *I* have to do with it?

He leaned toward her. He'd missed a patch on his cheek that morning, shaving, and the misaligned gray and black bristles looked like a mouthful of rotting teeth open and about to bite her. She resisted flinching.

Drawing you every day? he said. Your face? He stared at her, daring her to lower her eyes. She didn't.

He said, You think that's easy? You think that's *fun*? Even God had to do it only once. Then his voice calmed and he sat back and said, You'd be surprised how much a face weighs.

Which was strange to her, since her body had long felt weighted and heavy, stolid and imperturbable, whereas her face had always seemed as light as meringue. Perhaps that was because he had less and less power over her body as she aged. Her feet, yes, he could change those, and did, though she suspected that was due to his having done so when she was younger, yet the rest of it rarely seemed under his sway now, while he altered her face at will. She was just beginning to enjoy inhabiting her body (the times she didn't hate it), and for the first time, after his admission, it felt almost weightless.

This spurred her to recklessness the next morning when she came down to the kitchen to find it, once again, shiny with new things: famous oil paintings on the walls, a row of gleaming copper pots, huge ceramic bowls piled high with fruit (she especially loved the dusky pears). Her mother was putting away a new set of silverware and now they lay in their ordered ranks in the drawer, and yet both her parents seemed morose. Bernadette realized that these new things, which appeared at her father's behest, were the hinge on which her parents' marriage was based and that the hinge no longer worked.

You fill your lives with these new things, she said, but they don't make you feel happy, do they? They don't make you feel less small.

Her mother and father blanched, which meant she'd struck home, and she felt good, even as anger overtook her father and she knew she was going to pay for it, good until she saw her mother's hurt face, which crushed her. But she forgot about both that day at lunch, because her own features were so small she had to break her lunch into crumbs to eat it, though when she thought about it later in study hall (where she'd put her books aside because it was too much of an effort to read with such tiny eyes) she realized that her miniature features only proved her point. They were small, small people. And someday, she would be bigger than them.

•

Sophomore year, a day came when her father wouldn't get out of bed. Bernadette didn't understand why he was always so unhappy; if he drew things, they happened, and what could be better than that? So Bernadette banged two copper pots together over his head to wake him. He looked at her through one puffy eye, muttered something indecipherable into the pillow, and told her to leave him alone. She banged the pots together again before leaving, which felt gloriously transgressive, like sticking her tongue to a metal pole outdoors on a cold winter's day, the pain to come worth the intense present pleasure. (Or so she told herself.)

After fifteen minutes he came downstairs, but he just sat at the breakfast table in his bathrobe, hair sticking up as if he'd been electrocuted, and wouldn't pick up his pencil. He looked as though he'd been assaulted while sleeping, and Bernadette thought, *Old age is peeking over his horizon.*

The night before, her mother had been to the bakery, and now there were doughnuts on the table, chocolate with rainbow sprinkles, Bernadette's favorite, and she really wanted one.

I want a doughnut, she said. One of the odd things about it was she could talk without a mouth and see without eyes, though only around the house. She'd never figured out how that worked, but right now she didn't care; she wanted a doughnut and she needed a mouth to eat it.

Immediately, when his eyes went from her blank face to the doughnut and back, she wished she hadn't said a thing, hadn't clanged those pots together a second time, and as soon as he began drawing she felt her lips forming on her face and knew what he'd done without even looking.

You can't do this! she said, unable to keep her tongue from circling her thick, chocolate-frosted lips.

I already did, he said, and stomped back upstairs to bed.

Mom! she said, but her mother shook her head. She was looking rather vague these days and smelled kind of peaty, like whiskey. You know your father, she said, and lit a cigarette, an old habit she'd begun again. I can't do anything with him once he's made up his mind, and besides, you look cute with a dough-nut on your face. Not everyone could carry off that look.

So of course during homeroom, Brian Anderson, whom she'd had a crush on for three years (and who had failed to speak to her for the previous 1,147 days, a running count she kept in her notebook) said, Wow. That thing looks perfect for blowjobs, which made her burst into tears and run into the bathroom. Not even her best friend Cindy could get her to come out, and she got detention for a full week for missing all her classes. She felt especially bad that she almost liked that Brian had been cruel to her, because it meant she wasn't invisible.

The school had called, evidently, because her father was waiting for her when she came home, pencil at the ready, and before she even got a chance to speak he drew a big scarlet let-ter on the page, then a caricature of her around it, and she felt the D forming on her forehead.

It's not my fault, Dad, she said, and burst into tears, and for the first time she could remember, her father seemed surprised.

What happened?

She told him, and he erased the D (a little roughly, she thought, since she felt her skin burning, but she didn't think it wise to tell him), turned the page on his drawing tablet, and said, Who was the boy?

She couldn't bear the thought of Brian Anderson being made to look freakish, so she said, Gordy Cooper, who was a dorky boy in her class about to move. That week, in fact, since his mother had accepted a new job in Chicago.

What's he look like? her father asked. This Cooper kid?

I don't know, she said, shrugging. Like a pear.

All night she felt guilty, but she was relieved when Gordy wasn't in school the next day, or the day after.

But really, she didn't have much time to think about him, because her father had changed her mouth completely. That morning at breakfast her mother was whispering to her father about it, and as usual he was stubborn. No way, Bernadette overheard him say. I'm giving her a mouth that no boy will ever think about sticking a cock in. When her mother continued to object, he said, Think how much she'll save on lipstick, and for some reason that quieted her.

For a year and a half Bernadette lived with it. And in some ways, it wasn't all bad: the fangs didn't really come together when she chewed, which was uncomfortable, so she ate less and lost fifteen pounds and fit into clothes she never could have worn before. Cindy, who suddenly seemed able to gain weight just by breathing, gave Bernadette all the clothes she was growing out of, and now boys looked at Bernadette in a different way, as long as they got past her lack of lips. The only really bad part was that Bernadette had to unfriend Gordy Cooper, because on his Facebook page his picture was pretty much the same as always except his head, which was now a pear, sometimes with a single serrated green leaf sprouting from the stem. It made her feel guilty to look at it.

When she finally got her lips back and lost the fangs, it was by mistake. She needed money to buy a new hairband and her allowance was in the bank and her paycheck from the ice cream store wasn't for another week, so she was fishing for quarters under the seat cushions in the study when she found her father's stash of *Playboy*s.

That night at dinner her father had had a few scotches and she realized it might be dangerous to speak up, but she was tired of stuffing her anger.

Why are you always so unhappy? she said to her father.

He finished another scotch, rattled the ice cubes in the empty glass, and let out a long, theatrical sigh. Because I don't like to draw anymore.

Why not? she said. And if it's so bad, why do you do it?

He popped an ice cube in his mouth and sucked it for a long time while she waited for an answer. At last he said, Because the world exists to be drawn, and because you and your mother are expensive to maintain.

Having maneuvered him where she wanted, she said, Then draw me like this, and flipped open a *Playboy* to a picture of a brunette in jodhpurs with a pair of full breasts straining at her pink sweater.

Instead, the next morning he drew her with a big nose, long and pointed, like a sharpened broomstick.

Don't go sticking it in other people's business, he said, and sent her off. Her mother wasn't even coming out of her room anymore, so Bernadette didn't bother asking for her help.

He'd forgotten her left hand, but because he gave her a normal mouth and teeth by mistake, she didn't complain, though it hurt when she closed her nose in her locker and she was red-faced for half an hour after Brian Anderson said, Wow, you look like the Pinocchio and the prostitute joke. When others stopped to listen he said, Lie to me! Lie to me!

That doesn't make any sense, Brian, she said, not liking that he was the same mistake at seventeen that he had been at fourteen and fifteen and sixteen, liking less that she kept making it.

Who cares? he said. All I want is for you to lie to me!

With such a big nose, his cologne (which she'd never liked) smelled like a cleaning product, and she'd finally had enough, so she said, All right. Turn around and I will.

When he realized what she meant, he paled and pushed past her, and she poked him in the back with her nose as he reached the corner, drawing laughs. It felt good not to let him get at her, and she wondered why she'd ever protected him in the first place, and vowed to tell her father about Gordy Cooper that afternoon when she got home.

All day her nose kept getting in her way—it was really hard to eat with—so she went to the library at lunchtime and wandered through the stacks, pushing her nose against the spines of interesting books, eventually finding herself in front of the art section. At one point she stopped (she thought later it must have been fortuitous) because when she paid attention she was looking at the spine of a book on drawing caricatures; it took her several minutes, but she managed to pry it free with her nose and it dropped open on the floor to the very first page of instructions.

Why not? she decided, and got a paper and pencil and began to draw.

Start with the eyes, it said, not with the shape of the head, as that can be restrictive, and outline the nostrils with thick lines. It cautioned her to leave enough room below the nose for the mouth and to make the mouth lines thick (except for the bow of the top lip, which was to be very light) and offered tips on chins and cheeks and jaws, which were to be drawn in that order. The last sections showed her how to use squiggles, curves, and *v*'s, and how to shade and exaggerate the obvious.

Brian had a widow's peak, so the first person she drew, and for an hour the only, was Brian with a dormer on top of his head, but no matter how many times she tried, erasing, redrawing, shading lines lighter or darker, nothing happened to him as he sat across from her in history class, playing with his pen or snapping Cindy's bra. Still, she felt elated. Somehow, being forced to use her off hand—her right hand—made drawing easier. She drew Gordy Cooper as himself from memory, only with fewer freckles, on the off chance it would help.

For the rest of her classes she sat at her desk, ignoring Cindy's looks (at first pleading, and then angry), drawing everyone she could, convinced she was doing a good job: Mr. Hortmueller's huge jaw, Mrs. Strathmore's droopy ear lobes, Ms. Villanueva's tiny hands. Nothing, even when she gave Ms. Villanueva two extra pinkies. On Madame Hinault's big rear end it seemed to work— the seat of her pants suddenly expanded—but when she erased it and redrew it twice the size, nothing changed; it must have been her father, busy in his office, which made sense. Two o'clock: he'd be up at last, rushing to beat the syndication deadline.

Finally she gave up and put the book away.

That night at dinner, her father looked terrible, and when her mother asked what was wrong, he rubbed his forehead like he was sanding it with his palm and said, I don't know. A terrible headache. All afternoon, my head seemed to get larger and smaller.

It's not a stroke, is it dear?

I don't think so. Just a headache. And with that he went up to bed.

In her room, Bernadette drew with the door open as the evening light faded to darkness and then brightened again, in the brilliant silver bloom of the moon. No matter whom she drew, she heard her father toss and turn. Big ears, a massive chin, a nose in the shape of a menorah. Once she went in to check on him after she'd altered a drawing of Brian Anderson and her father had huge clown feet, almost up to the ceiling, and a flaccid face that sagged over the side of the bed.

Maybe it was just that she was young, she thought, and her power wasn't very general. Or maybe it was all she could ever hope for. Either way, it made her happy. She studied the last image—her father, older—turned out the light and went to bed.

In the morning, he was up surprisingly early.

I didn't want to stay in bed, he said.

Restless?

Headaches and bad dreams, he said. Most about the Barking Dog. I'd had enough of both of them. The skin on his face sagged, but it could have just been the way he was leaning on his slender fingers, she told herself; it wasn't necessarily the power of her pencil, though his newly swarthy skin she attributed to a bit of amateurishness on her part in terms of crosshatching. Too heavy; she'd have to use a lighter pencil next time round.

Bernadette made him breakfast, serving him tea instead of coffee. Dangerous, since he hadn't yet drawn her, yet she explained that it was supposed to increase blood flow through constricted vessels, which would relieve headaches, and he thanked her and quickly sketched her in. Almost normal, except for a vague patch on her jawline and a slightly lopsided left ear. She looked at herself in the mirror and thought, This'll do, especially when she smelled his lemony cologne and realized her nose worked perfectly.

The wind outside was enormous. Stoplights swung parallel to the ground, the speed-limit sign banged on its metal pole, and all the windows rattled in their frames. Perhaps that kept him up too, she thought, though really she'd been so involved with her drawing that she hadn't heard a thing.

Her father left the house and began his long daily walk—to clear his head, he claimed, leaning into the wind—and immediately she took out paper and pencil and drew his slanting, surging figure, exactly as it appeared. He paused, flickered, and moved on, and then she erased his ears.

He dropped his hat and began frantically patting his head until his hands were pushed away by huge, flowering ears, ears bigger than Dumbo's, bigger than billboards. They billowed in the gusting wind, stretched taut as she drew them, lifted him up and sent him sailing away over all the houses, feet kicking as if he were swimming toward the low full moon. The goddamn moon, she thought. It was the last she ever saw of him. And of

her mother, who, it turned out, existed only in her father's imagination and through the machinations of his pencil. Which, she
decided, meant she was half a figment too, and that explained
why she could exist (partially) without him.

After college, in his old notebooks and sketchpads, Bernadette
sometimes drew her father wandering through various familiar neighborhoods, but when she went there herself she never
found him. Everything else was exactly as she and he had drawn
it, lemon trees and striped children, slanting houses, blocks of
pastel apartments and expanses of purple lawn, even sprinklers
with miniature rainbows on summer evenings complete with
barking dogs chasing their own tails, but her father was present only in his absence, no matter how many times she sketched
him in; she simply couldn't conjure him. Mademoiselle Ample
Hindquarters remained amply rumped, Bernadette herself suffered through once-yearly gigantic feet, but her father wasn't
even a shadow beneath an awning. And as a result, she couldn't
recover her mother, either.

Eventually Bernadette began using her father's pencils (a
little harder than she liked, a little darker) and his paper only
to change her look from the one her father had left her (a different hairstyle, fuller lips, smaller or larger curves) and at first
she loved sitting at the breakfast table and trying on one face
after another, drawing herself from memory or from the mirror.
If she forgot, she couldn't have her coffee, so her mouth always
came first, and on Sundays, of course, she let herself go face-
less until noon.

But finally the need for constant invention grew wearying,
so she settled on a basic face that she altered when the mood
took her or on special days or anniversaries. When she had a
cold she made her nose a trumpet so all the neighbors would
hear her blow it, when she had a date, she spent extra time on

her eyes and lips, and in the middle of a bad or boring one, she'd go to the bathroom and take out a pencil and sketch paper and make her nose bigger or her eyes lopsided. One especially unendurable date (an hour's disquisition on salt and the body) caused her to draw her left ear in the shape of a salt cellar and to weigh down both wrists with enormous paper watches; it was a delicious pleasure to return to the table and watch her date struggle to understand what had happened. And when she really wanted to tease, she'd use a much harder or darker pencil in the bathroom, as those dented the paper, giving her jawline odd contours, and darkened her skin.

On her father's birthday, she would alter her face to look like something he'd once drawn for her, the big ears the time she wasn't supposed to be listening, a can-opener chin the time she had trouble with a soda bottle, the various buttons that had been her nose. Brass, pewter, tortoiseshell, cloth, shell and bone. Most were round, though some were oval, a few rectangular or square, one was shaped like a parenthesis, and now and then she mixed in the single star or the maple leaf or the miniature silver squirrel. On her seventh date with the man she was falling in love with, she switched her circular ivory nose to an oval ceramic one, to see if he would notice. He did, and rubbed it with his thumb as soon as she sat back down, making her shiver. That night in bed she fell back on her old skill at mimicry, saying her name in his voice over and over again until she at last fell asleep.

And of course she had her work. Her best-selling strip became *The Adventures of Miss Minnie B*, whose heroine was forever in search of her lost family (she'd become separated from them in a time of great struggle, left purposely vague). Like all such strips, Bernadette realized, it depended on Miss Minnie's endless striving and never arriving: readers would remain interested in her only as long as she never got what she wanted.

So, both Bernadette and her heroine would go on endlessly searching, thanks to her father. That was all right, Bernadette decided one morning as she sketched Miss Minnie B sitting at the very same breakfast table she herself sat at with Ribeiro, her love, her life, sitting beside her. Miss Minnie B's day-to-day life was a mirror in which she could view both her unchangeable past and her uncertain future, a strange gift from the closest strangers of all, her parents. And each day she awoke wondering what it would bring.

Betrayal

My mother liked mushrooms. Not the real ones. Glass, concrete cast to look like stone, papier-mâché. Two I remember especially were an amber orange and a Heineken beer-bottle green. I brought home one in purple-blue glass my third year in college and she said, Oh, I don't like them anymore.

They nestled on the wooden shelves between windows, the chestnut-brown wood marked with chevroned black water stains, as if from high tides, a beautiful house but poorly built. Sometimes I'd look out past them to the patch of sunlight where she sat in her lawn chair, drinking her morning drink: orange juice and whiskey. My first drink too, which tasted bitter and burned my tongue.

A year after the blue mushroom she sat in the lawn chair, crying, telling me she was an alcoholic. I'd just cut the grass. Its fresh smell tickled my nose, green blades clung to her tennis sneakers, and a long string of saliva and tears hung from her chin. *I will never drink again.* I said nothing. Why would I? I'd known for years, and, aside from anger, all emotions in our house were kept as thin as an unused envelope. Later, her muffled voice came through the study door; she was on the phone to her counselor. *I'm going away for rehab for a year and she doesn't have any reaction at all!* Later still, I heard her in the study again, opening the liquor cabinet, bottles clinking together, which became for me the sound of betrayal.

•

Often I walk at night alone in my neighborhood and look at the lighted windows. The houses aren't as beautiful as my childhood home, but better built. Behind which yellow rectangles are lives falling apart? Mushrooms are no clue; they grow on everything here in the South where the humidity dampens the world, sprouting from the sides of trees, from sidewalk cracks, from a piece of chipped brick outside our front steps. Where my husband is probably in the kitchen, taking another bottle of wine from the fridge. But since I'm out here I can't hear it clink against the mayonnaise and milk, which means it isn't really betrayal.

The Builder's Errors

They found her, or her body?

The voice on the phone had said something about peace, about closure.

Her body.

Then I thought, *Where* was *she?*

I set out to find out.

I collected everything of hers I could find: clothes and shoes, diaries, pictures, books, papers she'd written, notes, letters, emails, and all the recordings—her voicemail greeting, old videos, YouTube videos friends had made—everything. I drew up a life-size model and had it made, split down the middle and hinged, and put most of these things inside it, laid extra shoes by the feet, blouses and dresses beside her, turned the recordings into MP3 files which I downloaded onto her iPod, worked for months with a gnomish engineer to loop the videos on little screens which went into the face in lieu of eyes.

The dining room, the living room, her bedroom, the patio; in different moods I switched her to different rooms, but whenever I played the iPod I always put it on shuffle. For some reason hearing her sing Christmas carols outside always made me sad, though in the kitchen they caused me to smell the mulling spices and pour myself a glass of cold cider, while the sound of her snorting laugh as I stepped from the shower made me hard. Night or day, her giggles made me cry. All of it was good, I thought, all of it made me feel.

Still, none of that was *her*, not even at night when I lay down beside her and by chance she sang me a lullaby, the best of which had been recorded when she herself was young by her mother and played for me the first time I went to her house. Don't let the beebugs bite, she sang, so softly it was just a whisper. Not even when I fixed her arms in an embrace. So when I heard of the fiction project, I thought I'd give it a try.

I wrote stories. They weren't very good at first, takes on old fairy tales and books I'd read as a boy or she as a young girl, featuring her in one of the starring roles—the best one was as Little Red Riding Hood—but as they grew more sophisticated, I thought I saw glimpses of her now and again, running through the forest with bare dirty feet in warm twilight gloom, laughing as she splashed in the waves on a bright chilly day, angered at a friend, glaring at a retreating taxi's taillights on a wet, shiny city street. Still, that wasn't enough. I made movies, but in every shot I saw the same thing: *Not Her.* Late one night I realized the problem; they were *of* her, not actually her. So I went back to the stories where I'd glimpsed her and filmed them, from her eyes. Better, but not enough. Video games? She'd loved those, so I tried those too. Nothing. Back to the stories then, but they no longer worked; whatever magic I'd once found seemed to have vanished, perhaps because I'd betrayed them.

I started burying things. A favorite blouse, the brown and red and yellow sweater her great-grandmother had knitted for her, two papers on which she received her worst grades ever. Months later I dug them up and found them dirty and ruined, beginning to decay, fabric frayed, her teacher's red ink faded to brown; it didn't help. I took the shoes she'd been unearthed in, scuffed and battered and sagging, and carved two square openings in the plaster wall beside the living-room fireplace and put one in each and covered them with semi-transparent panels. You could see the shoes in outline but no detail, and the mystery of them invited you to look harder, to try and decipher exactly what was behind those imperfect windows. When I grew tired of the standing and staring in the enormous silence they engendered, I pried off one cover and put in the iPod and recovered it; when the battery died I left it in. I began haunting the library, where I read magazines and newspapers from the months before she died, trying to recapture my earlier mindset, to glory in upcoming movies that were already out on video, to speculate about the outcome of elections long over, to believe she was still alive, to lift or shift the dome I'd been living under.

Eventually I gave up and went through the usual modes of self-destruction: a lack of baths, poor nutrition, excessive drinking. My pores began to smell so much of bourbon that I could sniff my own forearms instead of pouring myself a drink. I quit that too.

I grew angry at the model, yelled at it, ignored it, and, a good hater, bit it once on the forearm, leaving teeth marks on the smooth plastic skin. I hid it then, inside a long cedar-smelling blanket chest, covering it with old costumes and heavy silver trays, as if afraid it would rise up of its own accord to haunt me. I knew I was burying it, I knew it wouldn't work. That night, worried about its open eyes playing the endless loops of her, I opened the chest and uncovered its head and tied one of the Hermès ties she'd given me for an anniversary in an orange and white blindfold around those flickering eyes, and after that I was able to sleep. For weeks and weeks I had peaceful nights, though I was never able to say at any single point in any given day that I was happy, that I'd been released.

Then early one bright winter morning—snow, the city quiet, the trees freighted with thick cotton, all sounds muffled, not even footsteps or tire tracks marring that undulating emotive blanket—I sat down and began to write.

They found him, or his body?

The voice on the phone had said something about peace, about closure.

His body.

It was strange feeling my hips widen, my waist narrow, my chest swell, watching my hands transform, the fingers shortening and slimming, rounding from their original forms, the nails growing longer and more manicured, strange too to realize that my hair now fell halfway down my back, but of course the internal changes were more profound. My grief felt like a horizontal tear in my chest rather than a huge weighted bolus in my stomach, and instead of desiring to box it up, to keep it trapped and echoing inside the frail, tensed border of my skin, I wanted to ladle it out to all who passed. I sought scents, the timbre of his voice, the pressure of his warm callused palm on my lower back, tense from a bad day at work, the rasp of his unshaven cheek on my thigh humid from the bath, an internal hum that alerted me to his presence. I could go to the cemetery openly now, instead of furtively.

I looked up for him and when a flock of chattering starlings exploded from a tree like a black firework against the blueberry sky, I began to weep and sob. He was never coming back, and I realized how much and how forever I was going to miss him.

Mum on the Rocks

I stood in so many lines to bring my mum back it wasn't even funny. I paid the broker's fees, I paid the transport costs and sales tax up front, I paid cabbies to ferry me all around town to the various offices I had interviews at, and even so I almost lost my job, because to get a return you have to be in the right offices during the right hours and if you have even a single stamp out of place on a single page of the application, or if you've gone to the wrong notary or miss just one appointment, you have to start the whole process all over again, and that can take years. Years! Something had to give, and in my case it was work. No promotions and no raises during the entire process, but I knew it was worth it. I mean, she was my mum. Who wouldn't want to bring their mum back from the dead?

Pretty soon after she came back, I had a better idea of who might not want to, and I began to wonder why there weren't blogs about the topic, or at least books. Couldn't someone have told you that whoever comes back from the dead is pretty much who they were before they died, except for one crucial difference: their single most annoying habit is magnified one hundred times? Something about the passage there and back, I guess. No one ever bothered explaining it.

Berkely's sister went to the bathroom ten times as often and still never flushed, my boss's husband sucked his teeth constantly (she said she was tempted to pop open the door to a 747 and jump out midflight to Japan after six uninterrupted hours of the squeak and smack of tongue, gum, and teeth), and my mum? She spoiled things. Movies, books, meals, she'd let me know ahead of time how they turned out. Eventually I learned to lie about what I was reading or going to see so she wouldn't tell me when the hero's brother died or that his wife developed amnesia or about the goofy ending, but I guess somehow the dead know the future too, which is how she could tell about meals. The artichoke salad I was making was going to cause heartburn and keep me up all night, the hamburger I craved from O'Falin's would give me diarrhea and make me miss a crucial meeting and lose a sale, the stuffed peppers Dashante hoped to bring by would give me a skin rash for a week. Even worse was that she could tell me about each new woman I brought home, or rather that she insisted on doing so.

Maude was a looker, but in ten years those looks would be gone. Imagine a muffin someone stepped on, she said. That'll be her face. Brianna liked to laugh now, and she was a better cook than she gave herself credit for, but down the road she'd be depressed for twenty years; did I really want to volunteer for a pair of cement overshoes? The red-headed lawyer I met at the company picnic had a sweet disposition but her liver would give out from all that vodka. Just remember, my mother said, that by forty her eyes will turn yellow, she'll look permanently suntanned, and at forty-five she'll be dead. Besides, she said, She's so full of it, her name should be Brown. It got so bad that after the last one (a blond pediatrician about whom my mother said, You choose that one, you're strapping yourself to a bomb, because even though she was smart and successful and passionate about politics and sports and loved to kayak and had the exact same sense of humor as me and dressed like a model, it turned out she was also going to end up sleeping with a series of pharmaceutical reps) I was tempted to stop coming over at all.

What? my mum said, looking hurt. You don't want me to save you heartache? Then what'd you bring me back for?

Under my breath, my hand on the blonde's back, I said I didn't know. Luckily, I was sure that the returned couldn't read your thoughts.

So the next time I went to see my mum, it was just me, angry and alone. *Better that way*, I thought, handing her a bouquet of fragrant hyacinths, hoping that the returned suffered from allergies, which would keep her worried about herself and not me. She lay the flowers on the counter while she searched the cabinets for a suitable vase, and when she found the curving bronze one she sat me down at the table, rested her free hand—thin and warm—against my cheek, and said, Good, I'm glad you're alone. Now I can tell you what's in store for you.

Geez Mum, no, I said, knowing. And I thought, *I'll get old, I'll die, if I have kids one of them might bring me back, and then it'll be my turn to annoy them.* I was wondering what my annoying habit would be when she surprised me.

No, she said, having read my thoughts. You're not going to have kids. This is your only go-round. But it's better that way.

What? Really? You can read my mind?

Yes, really, she said, misinterpreting one question and ignoring the other. I hadn't meant, *It's better that way?* but rather, *I'm not having kids? I don't get to come back?* It was an awful realization—my insides felt as if they'd just been cored and my heart seemed to have gone AWOL—but she just plowed ahead the way the returned will, as if those left behind are new ground that must be broken open again and again. I was wondering what my future was going to be like and why I'd never have kids, if I'd even marry, and she was already beyond that.

Yes, really, she said again, and patted my hand.

That hand pat was the clue, I realized later, what I should have paid attention to, a remnant of my childhood; when I was young and she patted my hand, the conversation was almost over. Soon, she would be up and on her way.

It's better, she said now, because if you did come back, you'd find that what time does to your kids breaks your heart. Believe me, she said, you don't want that. Of all the things in all of time, that's the worst of all.

Oh yes I do, I said, having to keep myself from shouting. I want a chance at everything.

No, really, she said. You don't. I promise. The second go-round's not as good as the first, just a pale pretense. Like an image of yourself dissolving in water.

Then—and I still don't know how she did it—she slipped her hand into the vase and once her fingers pierced the invisible rim they turned to water and her arm followed and she just kept going, pouring herself into that vase. When she was done her reflection trembled on the swaying surface, seeming to smile at me, before beginning to fade, slowly, slowly, slowly, just as she'd said, and I sat up half the night holding the vase, trying to call her back. Mum, I said, over and over, whispering, singing, shouting, pressing my face to its cooling side. When none of that worked I had to decide what to do with her. Letting the flowers soak her up seemed wrong, emptying her in the drain would feel sacrilegious, and flushing her down the toilet wasn't an option, but the longer I waited the more likely it was she would simply dissipate and float away on the anonymous air. I couldn't bear the thought of that either, so in the end I tipped her carefully into a dozen ice trays, and now she sits waiting for me in my freezer.

Sometimes at night after a long day at work I indulge myself, though I do so rarely to make sure she lasts. I turn off my phone and shut off the lights, so nobody driving by will think I'm awake and in need of company, call up a movie on Netflix and pop some popcorn and fix myself a drink and stretch out on the couch, my mother keeping me company as bits of her melt in the glass. Soon, at key points in the movie, she starts to talk from deep inside me, her sweet soothing voice echoing in my chest and ears, humming in my bones.

Watch this scene and pay attention, my mum says, warming the blood in my veins. He's going to kiss the girl and sparks will fly and you'll think they're going to last forever. But in the end, she says, they get it right. It doesn't work out.

Trapped in the Temple of Athena

You what? He turned his head to hear her over the raised voices in the bar.

Sell bones. Here. She leaned toward him, small breasts moving loosely beneath her filmy peach blouse, and he caught the citrusy bite of her perfume. Let me see your license.

She glanced at the back, snapped it against the zinc counter. Don't worry, you're safe with me.

Why's that?

Not an organ donor. She returned it, fingers lingering in his palm, and sipped her dark drink. He wanted to taste the smoky scotch on her tongue. She said, If I sleep with you, I won't be after your bones.

Sleep with me? he said. We just met.

But he shouldn't have been surprised. Braless, a semi-sheer blouse; she wanted to be noticed, though the charcoal-colored pencil skirt was knee-length and rather demure. Still, when she'd first sat down, a tall blond man moving away from the bar had bumped into him, staring at her, and spilled beer all down his sleeve.

She pulled out a business card and pressed her mouth to it, leaving behind an imprint of her full lips. *Aleka Chaltas, Bone Procurer.* He thought he recognized a Chanel shade, Rouge Allure.

Greek, he said, his voice not shaking. Long history with bones.

You've no idea. But if you're ever in the market, let me know.

So really, he said. What do you do?

Buy and sell. Hospitals, morgues, funeral parlors, from whoever doesn't need them to whoever does. Surgery practices too.

Did he make a face? She said, Don't worry. It's not so ghoulish as all that. Dental implants, hip replacements, spinal discs, you'd be surprised at the number of uses. Half the people in this bar either have them or will.

She had a tattoo, which he would have guessed, but not like this: a single rib, left side, second from the bottom, outlined in phosphorescent ink, which showed when she stretched her arms. Glimpsing it felt shockingly intimate, as if he'd walked in on her emerging naked and beaded from a shower.

She came back from the bathroom and stood between his knees, rested her cool palms on his hot thighs. Had she refreshed her perfume, or was he just noticing it again? He'd stopped responding to perfumes, he realized, though he must have smelled his girlfriend's every day.

Shall we go? she said. Standing this close, he understood her desire to be noticed was really a way to hide. If you were looking at her breasts, you weren't looking at *her*; he wanted to know what was behind the shield.

Yes, he said. Let's go.

It was too crowded to wait for the tab, all those bright hopeful faces jammed at the bar, so he put fifty dollars by their empty drinks and stood. All his cash. *Well*, he thought, *I won't need it.* They bumped through the boisterous crowd, Aleka in front, holding his hand, raising it like a drawbridge over shorter women who didn't move and taller men who wouldn't. Outside in the chilly dark the quiet was alarming, as if he'd gone deaf, and most of the lights in the surrounding buildings were out; Aleka took his arm.

Do you still have cash? she said.

His arm must have stiffened. Not that, she said and laughed. I'm *hungry*, and my money's at the hotel.

Can I walk you back? he said.

No, let's go to your place. I'll take a car in the morning.

At the ATM he withdrew two hundred dollars, but the first restaurant they passed was pulling down its metal shutters, so they began to run, laughing, her heels clattering. The shutters went down one after another, like stars winking out into darkness.

Winded, they walked and fell silent, pulled their coats more closely around them as they headed toward the river, its muddy musk growing stronger. The bars and restaurants died out, replaced by barber shops and hardware stores and old marine-supply shops, the buildings growing smaller and less well kept as they headed deeper into Butchertown, changing from stone to brick and from brick to wood. If they walked far enough, he thought, everything would be made of rubble and dirt, like some abandoned civilization slowly sinking into the earth. It was beginning to seem like a bad idea until they passed a small wooden church and he thought of his uncle.

I have an uncle, he said.

Everyone does.

You'd like him. Vinny stole bones. Italy, small town, a local church displaying the remains of a local saint. Bones and boots.

What saint? she said.

Vincent, he said.

Fate, then, she said.

Yes. Everything is. Free tickets to ball games, spaghetti dinners, archaeologists who die in cave-ins.

Even us?

Of course. And it was; his entire life had led to her. So, Vincent, he said. He was the saint of old women and lost shoes. My uncle, he goes nuts. Steals the bones and the boots. Two days later, they catch him—he's walking around in the boots.

Almost wore out that fifteenth-century leather, and the bones they never recovered. Put him in the local jail, the jailer goes off to fight a wildfire with a pick and shovel, when he comes back a week later, my uncle's dead.

Too bad he didn't know me.

Why's that?

I could have helped him with the bones.

And the shoes?

He'd have been on his own with those.

We're home, he said, and they were. She seemed startled and he was suddenly nervous, sweat prickling his groin. Here, he said, put your hands on this car.

What? Which one?

This blue one. One hand on each window. Press hard, he said.

Why?

But he watched her fingers straighten as she palmed the glass. It's my girlfriend's, he said.

Aleka shivered and said, And I thought *I* was strange. She dusted her hands on her skirt and said, You ought to clean it.

Her palm-prints glowed under the streetlight a ghostly white; he wondered what they'd look like by day.

Upstairs, she kicked off her shoes and went straight to the kitchen. His keys clattered on the counter against the others. Famished, she said. Haven't eaten all day.

Busy with work?

Busy with work, she said, obviously unwilling to talk about it. She pushed the keys around, flipping his and his girlfriend's, took down the olive oil and broke open a roll. What's your girlfriend going to say about all this?

She's not going to find out.

Her laugh was a single snort. Some of the oil she was pouring on the bread spilled; it shone on the top of her bare foot. He knelt to wipe it off, spreading a glistening streak over her pale arch.

Here, he said. Give me some more.

What are you doing? She spread her feet wider and looked down at him, roll paused near her open red mouth.

He held out his palm. Trust me, he said.

She poured the green liquid into his hand and he blistered it to warmth, then gripped her ankle and calf and began rubbing it in. His thumb traced the thin individual bones of her foot, her ankle, the stiff calf, the hollow at the back of her knee. Her tendons quivered. He had all the time in the world and some oil left and his hands kept rising. The smooth upswelling thighs—as beautiful as he'd guessed—and then under the skirt, where the fabric rippled over his knuckles as he massaged the oil into her buttocks. She gripped the counter and pushed back, arms stiff, elbows inverted. He slid his hands around front and worked the oil into the soft mound of pubic hair, pressing his cheek against her skirt. Her skin was warm, her muscles twitching; he smelled the sea.

They ended up back in bed, where, when she sat on him, gripping his shoulders with her toes, she kept slipping because of the oil. The loss of rhythm made them both giggle and she asked to switch around, but he insisted. Her nipples were darker than he'd have guessed; everything else about her was like Athena, but the truth was he needed to keep his hand on her waist to cover that glowing, tattooed rib.

After, he brought her water and they talked in the dark of the big city hospitals and small town morgues where she made her living. It's all marketing, she said. I have to be better and faster than the others.

The others?

The competition. You'd be surprised how many of us there are. And we're all a pretty devious lot.

Devious?

We change the dates on death certificates, to make them look younger, and if they died of cancer we change that too. Everybody needs bones, but they all want them virgin.

How do you get them to make the changes? he asked.

She was silent.

And what do they do? he said. I mean, how do they get them?

She put her hand on his sticky thigh. You don't want to know.

Please, I do. And he did.

The femur is best, she said, squeezing his thigh, because it's the longest. Tibia next, nice and thick—her hand was on his calf, moving out toward the shin—then fibula.

But why legs?

Easiest to cover up. Funerals. Open caskets? Almost never below the waist. But even if they are, you can replace the leg bones with PVC pipes, or broomsticks if there's no local plumbing supplier. Go in from the back so the surgery doesn't show, sprinkle expanding powder in and sew it up and you're good to go, forty-five minutes from first cut to last stitch. She reached behind him and ran a finger up the knobs of his spine, which made him shiver. And on really good cases, she said, we take this too.

She lay back and lit a cigarette, said, Will your girlfriend mind that I smoke?

No.

That snort of laughter again. You've done this before.

He didn't owe her anything, not really, but nonetheless he gave her the truth. Never, he said.

The radiators clanged, giving off their dusty heat, set on high because that's how Ath had always liked them, and Aleka told him the worst parts then—about how some crews toss their aprons and tools in the bodies before sewing them up, in order to hide what they'd done, how they peel off the skin and bag it, since skin comes at such a premium—the cigarette glowing in the dark like a flare. Career opportunities for cadavers, she said, a line that sounded both practiced and protective, that came from a desire to place herself at one remove from what her job required, and he knew that her flip talk sprung from sadness, from being appalled at what we did to one another, the living and the dead. Which explained the undercurrent of mournfulness that followed her like a perfume, the transparent blouse.

The cigarette hissed out when she dunked it in the water and she didn't say another word; soon she fell asleep. He couldn't, legs tingling where she'd traced his bones, and he got up and opened a package of pajamas Ath had bought for him. Long pants, long sleeves. He knew he'd sweat in the heat, but he was unable just then to bear the thought of being naked, simply a body.

He woke to soaked sheets and an empty apartment, the silence of absence, not quiet. Downstairs on the street, six a.m. and the fruit trucks out, garbage ripe on the chilly morning air, one woman walking home in a single shoe, blouse hanging from her rumpled red skirt. Ath's car was gone. *I'll take a car.* He laughed. He hadn't been sure what he was going to do with it.

Back inside he checked his wallet and was relieved and disappointed to find the cash. Tucked where Aleka's card had been was a folded note. *You snore. How does your girlfriend sleep?*

How much of what she'd told him was true? A little or a lot, it didn't matter. He refolded the note, creasing it tightly like Ath would, imagined her long nimble fingers running its too short length. His eyes stung and his throat thickened; he was glad he didn't have to speak. *She sleeps like Vinny,* he thought, and wondered if all her bones were with her when they closed the lid.

Lands and Times

We were all struggling with our inheritances. The problem is, they don't read the wills anymore, so we had to wait the entire meal for everything to come out. This was on a Monday, the moon's day. None of us spoke much as we sipped at our caldo verde, the olive oil shining on its placid green surface, but during the salad course João and Fatima dropped their forks at the same time—the heavy silver forks Mamãe had inherited from her avó—and as they clunked and clattered against the table Papai had made, João and Fatima turned their hands over and sat staring at their palms.

These *thumbs*, they said, and we knew; Papai was famous for his fumbling thumbs.

Conversation got loud then; we dug into the oiled tomatoes, the raw onions, the smooth, trout-colored olives, chattering excitedly; it was as if we could relax, knowing the process had begun, and we were anxious to see what was next.

Soon Afonso's voice stood out from all the others; it sounded peculiar through his new nose. And to be honest, the nose looked funny on him, overgrown and pocked. Papai's childhood illnesses had marked him, and though he never said so we knew he was ashamed of his nose. That mustache! I felt it sprouting on my face during the meal, and I was surprised how much I liked it. I'd have to wax it, but Mamãe could show me how to do that. She'd been doing it for Fatima for years, something I'd always oddly envied. Perhaps my hair would thicken now, like hers. After every bite I dabbed my lips with the embroidered napkin, so I could touch it with my fingertips.

By the time we got to the bacalhau and cream, three pairs of eyeglasses soaked in glasses of mineral water. I was glad Mamãe was still in the kitchen; that was one thing she wasn't going to like. I could tell Luisa had got the eyes; like me, she was peering at her food as if it was peculiar. Everything on my plate looked like sardines. *How long would that last?* I wondered. Only when I brought the food to my mouth could I tell what it was: chicken piri piri, Papai's favorite. My eyes brimmed, and though I could have said it was the chilies, I didn't let the tears fall; he would have been proud.

Mamãe came out of the kitchen, her hands coated with flour. Behind her floated the caramel smell of her rich, dark coffee; the bica cups would be lined up on the counter. But she was still making the cake, which was unusual; she had always been finished with everything ahead of time. Grief. They'd fought enough over the years, but we'd always known they couldn't get along without each other. Their fights seemed almost choreographed, like something a comedy team would put together, so how could she not be lost without him? He should have been yelling from the head of the table, asking her what was wrong, and she should have been yelling back that her only problem was that one day she'd met him.

She pushed through the swinging door and stood looking at us, her hands to her face, flouring her skin, making herself a ghost. And it must have been a shock. We'd had the whole meal to get used to the changes, after all, and here she was taking them all in at once.

What's wrong with you, Issabell said, and Mamãe covered her ears. I didn't blame her. It was strange to hear Papai's voice in Issabell's throat, stranger still that Issabell used his exact same words. But when Mamãe took her hands away, her ears were gone. I looked across the long table at Luisa, and there they were, sprouting from underneath her long hair. So big, with those oval, pendulous lobes! Oh, I was terrible: the first thought that crossed my mind was, *Now she'll get Mamãe's earrings too*. I studied her, feeling guilty. Until that moment, I'd never noticed how much she sat like Mamãe, the rounded shoulders, as if her shawl was really a boulder.

Mamãe got really angry.

Not even dead yet and you're taking everything from me!

Her cheeks were gone now too—Jaime had those, puffy and sagging, which wasn't a surprise, since he'd always been fishing quarters from the bottom of her purse, tobacco flakes clinging to his sweating palms—but Jaime's cheeks were lineless. Who'd got her face's little broken blood vessels? No one around the table had them.

Mamãe turned on me.

You! she said. You! I never figured it would be you. The others, yes, but not you.

I wanted to say something but I was ashamed. She had enough to handle with Papai's death. I put my hands to my warm, blushing skin, but I couldn't feel them, so I picked up my spoon and checked out my swollen, upside-down reflection, and if I looked closely—I had to learn to focus with the new eyes—I could see the spidery lines. What were they? Capillaries? Venules? Arterioles? I couldn't remember. But why not? It seemed only yesterday Papai had been quizzing me for my anatomy and physiology class. Then I remembered that he'd forgotten them as he aged—our body game became a chore in all my later visits—and realized I must have inherited his memory. I sat quietly, searching, and sure enough, there were all his older brothers and sisters, the ones who'd died long before I'd been born, whose faces I'd never seen except in my imagination and whose names all of us bore. It was a surprise to learn that the first Issabell had green eyes. Often in the fall Papai used to stand on the back porch at sunset and stare east, and now I knew I'd been right all along; he was looking toward where they lay in the still earth. Then an odd thing happened: I remembered two he'd never even mentioned. Who were they? I had so many new memories to begin to forget! It saddened me, so I concentrated on the reflection of my face again; all those tiny red lines made it look like a road map of rural Connecticut. Seemingly angered by it, Mamãe pushed through the swinging door back into the kitchen.

The musky scent of Papai's cologne drifted across the room, growing stronger. Afonso. He seemed to have rolled in it, which surprised me. Afonso had always been the reserved one; now it seemed he was making some kind of statement, which of course made sense. We'd all been changed by our gifts. As if to prove my point, Issabell began to speak. Normally she was as quiet as paint, but now she began to tell a long story about the tan and indigo ceramic teapot with the complicated, double-notched lid that had long been Mamãe's favorite gift from him, and it was like hearing the walls speak, only with Papai's voice. She told how he'd stolen the teapot from a china store in Hamburg one year when he was young and on leave from a freighter, how he'd carefully hidden and guarded it aboard ship, terrified not that he'd be found out but that he'd be stolen from in turn. She had to tell the story quickly, before Mamãe reemerged from the kitchen, and as she did, I was remembering the story seconds before she told it, the details that appeared in my mind blooming in her mouth. From now on, I realized, Issabell and I were going to be more closely connected than ever, for if I had Papai's memories, she had his voice, and what I remembered, she would give voice to. Another gift from the dead.

At the end of his tale I felt immense relief, the guilt Papai had carried with him all these years at last beginning to dissipate, but since I felt yet did not think it, Issabell did not say it. My new memories would be ours, but my new feelings only mine. Selfishly, I decided to keep them to myself, or this one at least, for now, even as I watched all my siblings with their new eyes and thumbs and noses begin to sag in their seats. Papai a thief! He wasn't quite the papa we remembered.

No, I thought. *He was more.*

I worried Issabell would say as much, but of course it was my thought, not Papai's, so I smiled and reached for the teapot (which seemed to have turned untouchable for everyone else) and poured myself more tea, glad as I picked up the unmatching tea cup that my thumbs were still my own and I would never have to worry about dinner-table clumsiness, and greedy to keep this bit of Papai to myself.

I felt a chill. Under the table my feet were suddenly bare. What was going on? Duarte was smiling up at me, my son. A bit unsettling still, since the teeth were much too large for his mouth, though of course his grandfather had no use for them now, but he was standing in my shoes. As I watched, his feet and ankles began to swell. I had to laugh. A boy in pumps! I laughed so hard—not Mamãe's laugh, not Papai's, and not my own—that my cheeks shook, and I felt the tiniest of blood vessels bursting in them, the touch of a thousand ants, pinhead blotches that would show up like towns on that Connecticut map, new towns with ancient names. Nineveh and Babylon, Jericho and Jerusalem, Tyre and Sarepta, Alexandria, Corinth, Rome.

Separate Love

The dog show seemed peopled by two types, those serious about the sport and those in hopes of finding a companion, and Gwynn fell into the second group, where few were under the age of sixty. It saddened her to think she might be as obviously lonely as so many she saw, the men wearing the same suits they had twenty years before, cut for longer limbs and more muscular necks, the women overly made up, their dyed, depthless hair a series of unnatural colors: licorice-black, wood-shaving blond, the strident red of dried peppers. She was glad her own hair was its natural silver and that her makeup was understated—she'd never gotten used to the American fear of aging—and yet she understood why people fought against it; loneliness was a terrible gnawing thing that age only intensified. As she slipped through the perfumed crowds in search of Terry, half-listening to the muffled announcements from the crackling loudspeakers, she began to feel that perhaps everyone else had been right to try and alter their appearance—they all seemed so much more confident than she did—but then, rallying, touching each of her sapphire earrings for luck, she told herself that perhaps it was simply a matter of circumstance; they were in their element and she was not.

She hardly knew Terry, and she was a bit abashed to have pinned such extravagant hopes to so slim a tether. They'd reached for the same bottle of mustard at the grocery store, one she recognized from England from years before and had been surprised to see again. It still had the same silver and gold competition medals clustered on its yellow label and a centered crimson seal denoting its standing as the only royally procured mustard. The label *she* remembered, however, had been stretched across large square tins in her mother's kitchen, while this one was shrunken to fit the swollen confines of a stubby brown bottle. *Ah well*, she thought, making a joke of it, *such is the passage of time, nothing to complain about*; she herself had shrunken some too. At that moment Terry's hand had brushed against hers, a beautiful one, with long slim fingers and tanned smooth skin, and goosebumps shot up her arm.

He apologized and reached her down a bottle and they talked, Terry asking her so many questions that she'd grown flustered. How long she'd lived in Louisville, where she'd been before that, the source of her marvelous accent; no one had paid her that kind of attention in years. Twice, he touched her elbow. His beautiful cashmere sweater, his flat stomach, his basket filled with fresh fruit and exotic spices, it was thrilling to meet someone her own age still so curious and so attuned to the senses, even as it made her feel a bit ashamed to have let recent years go by with such little effort. The one thing he revealed about himself was that he'd be attending the dog show—he did every year—and she'd come in hopes of seeing him again.

The fairgrounds were on the south side of the city, a sprawling complex of low steel-sided warehouses and a central brick pavilion moated by parking lots filled with campers and trailers. In the distance, the twin black-and-white spires of Churchill Downs poked into a slate sky over a neighborhood of brick apartments and two-family homes, like steeples in an Old Dutch painting. She'd driven through the area on her way, a section of Mexican restaurants and grocers and bars, Spanish signs hanging in the windows, aqua-colored walls, dolls wearing massive sombreros. Before this, she'd seen only a trickle of Hispanics in Louisville, men who came into her neighborhood rarely—to

cut lawns and trim trees and replace roofs—and here, she discovered, was the warm beating heart that pumped them out.
Louisville was a city that gave up its secrets slowly.

She'd concentrated on what she'd learned, trying not to get
her hopes up but growing more excited each time she urged
herself not to, so that by the time she parked in the jammed
lot and joined the crowd streaming toward the entrance, her
rapid breathing made her feel as if she'd run for miles. Her
heart would not be governed by reason. She'd had to stop and
willfully control her breathing, rocking in the steady wind, but
now, with the show half over and her ears buzzing from the too-
loud loudspeakers and her head dizzy from the scents of popcorn and dog urine and unfamiliar perfumes, that anticipatory
excitement had faded to a dull glow, coals gleaming beneath
ash. Terry was nowhere in sight, he'd spoken to her for a few
minutes at the grocers, they hadn't exchanged numbers or
agreed to meet; what on earth had made her seek him out? She
was too old to believe in fate, and he, it seemed, was too old to
remember all of his engagements.

She stopped at a station where a short-haired dog stood on
a judging table, tail erect, legs rigid, manicured muzzle tilted
to the auditorium's white rafters. Intelligent eyes, a well-pro-
portioned chest and torso, a shining, brindled coat—she wondered what type it was. Some type of hunting dog, perhaps; she
wished she knew. There was so much to learn and so little reason to learn it; she wouldn't come back on her own.

She was about to give up when someone tapped her shoulder with a rolled-up program and she turned to find Terry beam-
ing behind her. Surprise! he said. After he adjusted his yellow
bow tie—a detail that surprised her—he took her hand in both of
his and squeezed. That smooth skin, that all-encompassing attention, she was so happy to see him that it was a moment before she

found her voice and when she did she hadn't the heart to tell him
that their meeting was anything *but* a surprise. That would come
later, she imagined, shifting her strappy shoes free from a scrum
of popcorn, when they knew each other better and could both
look back with laughter at their first awkward meetings.

Forgive me for saying so, he said, but I know this show
inside out. If you'd like a guide, I'd be happy to help.

They made their way between sawhorses and vendor carts,
hips bumping as they passed through a picket-fence gate, sliv-
ers of pleasure surging through her stomach at the touch. Look
at that Weimaraner, he said, pointing his program to one standing nearby. What a magnificent coat.

It was, it shone like porcelain.

They came to a judge inspecting a Chow's feet, a tiara
of sweat glistening on his bald head beneath the lights. Terry
stopped and whispered in Gwynn's ear, lips brushing her skin
like a kiss.

He's the hardest judge here. If a dog has anything wrong,
anything, he'll find it. Watch, he said, a bit more loudly.

The judge expertly applied pressure to the back of the dog's
knee, causing it to raise its paw, which he poked and prod-
ded with a broad thumb. Have its pads been like this long?
he asked. Struck dumb, the owner could only twist her num-
bered armband on the sleeve of her pink blouse and shake her
head, glasses flashing in the light. Gwynn wished she could say
something to comfort her, but what? Years had gone into the
moment, no doubt, and now it was over, dreams crushed before
they'd bloomed.

They went on, Terry as voluble about the dogs and the
judges and the various events and the rigid order of seating in
the bleachers as he had been curious about her a few weeks
before, and the obvious pleasure he took in it all made him
even more attractive; she almost didn't want to admit to herself
how much. As they passed the booths and circled white judg-

ing rings, Terry identified some of the more obscure breeds with dizzying speed, the unruly Otter Hounds, the crafty Clumbers and Spinones, the mop-like Komondors and sturdy Kuvaszes, the reserved Airedales, the wily Dinmont Terriers, so many she couldn't keep them all straight. Standing under the hot lights she decided it didn't matter and that the dizziness was strangely comforting; she was falling into someone else's world—complete and accepted—in a way that she hadn't in years. Its rules and certainties were more than she could figure out in a short time, but clear enough that for now she wouldn't have to think too carefully, and that an immediate future spent sorting out their peculiarities would be thrilling. Her shoes tapped down the portable steel ramp as she followed Terry to the main floor, though she felt as if she were floating.

It had been a while since she'd met a man so alive to things other than the failings of his own organs. Many others her own age in the city were no doubt like him, but they tended not to congregate at the places she'd frequented, the JCC with its whirlpool and steam room, lectures at the library or museum, symphony matinees or an occasional bridge game at the Y; all of those seemed to attract the odd and the ill. The healthy were coupled off in houses, at parties, at evening concerts, at dinners and the theater, or, if single in those settings, not easily approached. In the last few years, the rare times she'd guessed correctly that an attractive man was single, she hadn't dared introduce herself, fearing that in doing so she'd signal some essential oddity and drive him away.

Backstage, people were chalking their Collies and spraying Toy Poodles with hairspray, puffing up the balled fur at their ankles and throats.

Oh look, Terry said, stopping so abruptly that Gwynn's breast pressed against his elbow. A Portuguese Water Dog.

It stood on a white table, large and curly-haired, about the size of a Standard Poodle, and not particularly distinguished-looking, the head large and too square, the muzzle thick, the tail bobbed.

It's the only dog in the world that can jump into a boat from the water without any help, he said. Fishermen use it to get things from the shore.

The working dog group, then? she asked.

Yes! His brown eyes opened wider with genuine pleasure. Very good! I've seen them do it myself at Faro, a whitewashed fishing village in the Algarve near where Prince Henry the Navigator sent off all those daring sea captains. Cabral, Dias, Da Gama, even Christopher Columbus. An entire carton of cigarettes, which he kept dry the whole way out. Eight hundred yards he must have gone, through four-foot waves. Their feet are webbed, just like a duck's.

May I see the dog's feet? Gwynn asked the owner.

She hesitated, shifting her braid from one thin shoulder to the other until Gwynn stroked the dog, its fur surprisingly springy and dry, and it nuzzled her hand in response.

Yes, Gwynn said, bending closer. You're a good girl, aren't you?

The woman's smile shifted her plain, red face into something almost welcoming. She likes you, she said. She doesn't like too many people. Here.

The woman's T-shirt rode up, revealing a crimson-and-gold butterfly tattooed across her lower back that reached to her pointy hips. Gwynn wondered if girls elsewhere had them as well, or only in America. As a child, the only two people she'd known to have tattoos had both been in prison. She took up one of the paws in her small hands and spread the toes on the thigh of her white jeans, and sure enough, there between the tightly wound fur was a black stretchy substance like the webbing on a duck's foot.

Gwynn squeezed it between thumb and forefinger. It's like canvas, she said. After Gwynn let it go, the dog put it up for Gwynn to hold again.

You must have a way with dogs, the woman said. I've never seen her do that for nobody.

Terry smiled at her. You really *are* good with dogs, aren't you?

Perhaps. It's been a while. I had one as a child. A Corgi.

You should get another one. He touched her arm and held it, just above the elbow. They're wonderful company.

That's good, she said, feeling her blood pulse beneath his fingertips, her skin grow warm. Good company is hard to find.

As they left, Gwynn heard one of the women talking to her dog. Flat ribs and open feet, what does he know? You're beautiful. She bent over to pet it and the hairbrush tucked into her waistband fell out and she started sobbing.

From the floor by a polished concrete ramp leading to a smoky tunnel, they watched the judging of the sporting group. We won't get to see everything if we're in the bleachers, Terry told her. You have to be up close.

Halfway through he excused himself and came back a few minutes later carrying two plastic cups of wine. In the interim three dogs had been paraded around the ring for the judge, their trainers taking dog treats from their own mouths to spur them on.

Sorry about these, he said, holding the sweating cups. But the wine is good. If you close your eyes and drink it, you can imagine you're somewhere more beautiful. One of the outdoor shows in the spring or summer, Charleston perhaps, or Savannah.

She held up the offered cup and said, Something to look forward to.

He smiled and nodded, seeming to catch her meaning. Do you have a favorite? he asked as the dogs paraded by, each swiftly circling the oval.

She sipped the cool wine and tried to view them all with a critical eye, the stride, the coat, the angle of head and tail, the way they responded to the brief commands. Not the Pointer, she said. There's something off about its proportions.

Yes. Exactly. A certain throatiness, the roached back.

They circled once more. The audience was silent, as if watching an aerialist perform an exceptionally dangerous stunt without a net.

The Gordon Setter, she said at last. Usually they look too thin and rather vacant to me. Overbred. But that one seems to have a lively intelligence. See how he follows his trainer's hands? He paraded beautifully while you were gone.

You've been watching, Terry said. Good for you.

But? Gwynn asked, hearing the hesitation in his voice.

But I'm afraid you've not picked a winner. At least not this year. You're right about them being overbred. That stigma's hard to overcome, and this is his first show. Maybe in another year or two. My money's on the Cocker Spaniel.

No! It seemed stout and unresponsive.

Yes. I know. He doesn't look as good as the Gordon. But he was second last year, and this year his competition is gone. It's like figure skating that way. How they did in the past can determine the present.

In the end Terry proved correct; the Cocker Spaniel was awarded the blue ribbon and the Gordon finished out of the running.

Fourth, though, Terry said, bending toward her to make himself heard over the applause. In two years, he might get the ribbon.

I'd like to see that, she said.

He dropped his cup in an overflowing orange trash barrel and took her elbow. Me too. In the meantime, how about if you come back to my RV? I've got something there I think you'll like.

She almost laughed at the old line, transformed only slightly by the switch from apartment to RV, until she realized he was serious, at which point she coughed into her cupped hand to buy herself a few seconds and finished her wine and thought, *Why not? In for a penny, in for a pound.* At least he hadn't said he wanted to show her his etchings.

Smoke and stale hot dogs and the sharp tang of urine in the tunnel out of the auditorium, a discomfiting reminder of the Tube, which always made her miss home; she breathed shallowly, trying not to inhale the unpleasant mixture. Halfway through the tunnel her uneasiness increased, as Terry had begun to ask her questions, his voice echoing oddly, and this time around the questions depressed rather than elated her: *How long had she lived in Louisville? And Florida before then? Was she English? Welsh? Why had she ever left home?* All things he'd asked in the grocers; she seemed to have been unmemorable. Even so, she struggled to keep her hopes up. Near the end of the tunnel the wind tugged at her skirt and the air turned refreshingly sharp; she breathed deeply to clear her nose and as she leaned into the stiff wind, hair whipping against her eyes, she realized it brought another blessing: conversation became impossible, which meant Terry couldn't ask her questions she expected him to already know the answers to.

She paused before the RV's three steep steps, then made herself climb them without a wince, determined not to allow a sore hip to make him think her fragile. He didn't notice her hesitation, or if he did, didn't comment on it. While Terry tried to calm a barking dog she patted her hair straight and set her purse on the demi-lune table by the door and knelt to rub the dog's ears.

It's a Miniature Shepherd, Terry said. Bred from a Shepherd and a Miniature Poodle, and so unusual we can't sell it to anybody.

Gwynn glanced casually around the room, wondering what *we* meant; there didn't seem to be signs of a woman. No purse, no scarves, no lipsticks on counter, table, or chair, and the decorating magazines stacked precisely on the coffee table and the matching candles flanking an empty cut-glass vase on the kitchen counter seemed to indicate a masculine sense of order.

The dog was six years old, no taller than an ottoman, with a bushy black tail and oddly colored for a Shepherd, yet attractive for all that, with an intelligent face and a thick, feathered coat. It licked her palm and sniffed at her shoes and jumped on the plush couch with its green brocade and large red roses and settled, turning twice before lying down with a snort. The exquisite fabric, the tastefully underdone décor, she told herself she had no reason to think all that meant a woman; Terry's own clothes were superb.

He announced that he was an Anglophile, but she'd already guessed it. Plates hung on the walls above the English country furniture, embossed with English castles, and between them were needlepoint royal crests in plain wooden frames. The complex House of Windsor's, the Tudor rose, even the vibrant tartan of the Stuarts. I did those, Terry said with obvious pride, nudging one corner of the Tudor straight with his thumb.

Your accent attracted me right off, he said, and I was *so* glad to see you tonight, to know that I was going to hear that wonderful voice again for an entire evening.

She flushed with pleasure and sat as he brewed tea, not minding that her apricot-colored sweater and midnight blue skirt, cut knee-length to show off her legs, were attracting dog hair like magnets. Terry brought her the steaming tea. All that's in stock, I'm afraid. I hope you don't mind.

I'm sure it's fine. What is it?

Raspberry.

Oh.

Not good? He pulled the cup back.

No. It's fine. Really. She reached out for it.

What, then?

I had an elderly patient once who'd drink only raspberry tea.

Was he impossible?

No, no, it wasn't that at all.

She told his story. He'd served with the Royal Welsh Fusiliers in Korea—her father's old regiment—and during one of the war's winters they'd gone months at a time with frozen wells and without water deliveries. No sense in it, really, she said. By the time it got to the front it was frozen and they had to thaw it out anyway, so they just cut ice from shell holes and melted *that*. They'd been using one shell hole for a week when they found eight bird feet. Then the birds themselves, pigeons, then boots, and when they chipped further the legs attached to them. A bird fancier, it turned out. He must have gone past their trench in the dark and fallen in the shell hole and drowned. Anyway, she went on, that put him off tea for a long time, though not forever. The habit was too strong, you see. So he switched to raspberry, since they'd never had that at the front.

Well, Terry said. *That's* a story I can't top.

It *is* rather strange. Sorry, she said, and rubbed her hand over one of the red roses. I hadn't thought of it in years.

I doubt it'll be long before I do, again, he said, and laughed. After a slight awkward pause the dog barked again and Terry began talking about him.

I've never had one smarter, or better behaved. Once I left a roast on the kitchen counter while I answered a phone call. He sat and watched it for half an hour.

Goodness, she said. That's more patient than *I'd* be.

Me too. He leaned forward and touched her thigh, just below her hemline. Secretly, I think he was hoping it would jump down so he'd be justified in attacking it.

Her skin tingled when he removed his hand, as if he'd stripped off a bandage, and over the next few minutes she managed to bump his knee twice with hers, signaling, she hoped, that she didn't mind his touch. Yet listening to the drift of his conversation she began to realize that she'd been brought in not as romantic interest or even as budding friend—something else, she thought, but just what she couldn't define—and when she caught herself clicking her silver bracelets together as he talked she made herself stop; perhaps there was still a chance. He refilled her teacup and the first sip scalded her tongue and she was grateful for the distraction.

Fifteen minutes later, Terry's friend Norm entered the trailer without knocking, removing his homburg and bowing slightly when he saw her, and she stifled a laugh, understanding at once the situation between the two of them and how wildly she'd miscalculated. Quickly she felt foolish and hollow.

Norm asked her if she'd enjoyed the show. Terry tells me it's your first.

Not as much as I expected to, she said, and immediately regretted it. Turning the teacup handle from one side of the saucer to the other, she vowed not to let her own hurt feelings bubble up again. Still, as the two talked, facing her, hips almost touching, a sadness settled in her stomach, a weight so heavy that it seemed she would never again be able to rise. A fancy, she knew. The one undeniable thing about unendurable loneliness was that it continued to be endured. It would have been better if she'd remembered that earlier and not come out at all.

Finished with her tea, she pushed the saucer away and stood, smoothing her skirt.

This has been wonderful, she said, but I really have to go.

Please stay, Terry said, remaining seated, which she appreciated, as it meant he really didn't want her to leave.

I'd love to, but I can't. She rubbed her hands together. Plans for tonight.

Lucky you, Norm said. No one invited us anywhere.

Terry scowled at him and stood with a sigh. Well, if you *must* go. But it was delightful having you here.

Gwynn, Norm said, walking to the door, I no longer have room for the dog.

I'm sorry to hear that. He seems nice.

He *is* nice. Which is why you *have* to take him.

Gwynn stopped. But I don't want a dog.

Terry touched her shoulder. You're a natural with them. I saw you.

I can't, really, she said. Nonetheless, she found herself standing with it at the foot of the trailer stairs while both men ignored her protests, Norm waving the homburg in farewell, saying over and over again how sweet she seemed as Terry smiled and wished her luck. When she tried to give the dog back, he handed her a stack of papers.

These are for the dog.

Oh. Norm reached around Terry and took them back. You won't need those.

She might, Terry said. If she ever has to take him to the vet.

She's got enough to carry already, with the dog, and with this. And with that, Norm handed her a ten-pound bag of dog food. That'll be plenty to get you started. The papers would just weigh you down.

Their faces blurred and she turned away, but they wouldn't have noticed. The door slammed and the RV rocked as the two of them climbed the stairs. Their shadows crossed the shade over the glowing window and came to rest side by side on the banquette and the dog looked up at her, wagging its too long tail.

The expectancy on its face was a mirror she didn't want to gaze in, too similar to what she herself must have looked like just hours before, and she banged on the door several times to get their attention. They ignored the noise and she began to feel foolish, fearing that she looked like a scorned woman to pass-ersby, and decided to take the dog to a shelter.

It leaned into her touch when she patted it, sending a sur-prising bolt of affection surging through her stomach, and she told herself that all the shelters would be closed at this hour so close to New Year's Eve and that she should take him home overnight, and when she realized she'd thought of the dog as *him* instead of *it*, she knew she wasn't going to abandon him. She couldn't explain it beyond the fact that he'd laid his head in her lap just at the point Norm sat across from her and put his hand on Terry's knee. Norm seemed to have intuited that she'd imagined her own delicate hand might rest there someday; when he caught her looking, he winked and flexed his pudgy fingers. His proprietary air made her feel as though she'd been kicked; worse, that she'd been meant to. Someone so cold might not hesitate to put down an unwanted dog.

Flags snapped above the arena in the whipping wind and the rain started, fat cold drops spotting the pavement; the first ones struck her face. She ducked instinctively and turned away, the dog trotting beside her as she hurried to her car to beat the onset of the full storm, ashamed of the profligacy of her own heart.

Balloon Rides Ten Dollars

From the funeral parlor porch I saw the sign BALLOON RIDES TEN DOLLARS and thought, *Why not?*

The balloons, bright and bobbing back and forth in the field across the road as if floating on a huge, slow sea, glowed against the dimming sky.

I walked through the beaten grass to the nearest, a yellow and gold affair with an affable woman about my mother's age in the basket. Beside it another, much younger woman and her small child were standing oddly, toe to toe, blond head to blond head, holding each other's hands but leaning backward with their rear ends, so they made a set of unequally sized parentheses. I thought of my own mother, dead these seventy-two hours, and wondered if we'd ever stood in such a fashion.

Ten dollars? I said.

What?

Ten dollars? I had my wallet out. For the ride?

The woman in the basket blinked. Oh, yes, that's right.

I handed her a ten and climbed in. The basket smelled of the oily fuel.

How long will the ride be? I asked.

Ten dollars, she said, and reached down for a sandbag, which she levered over the side.

There were three more. I thought I should explain about my back, so I did.

No matter, she said, bending to retrieve another.

After she tossed the last one, the balloon began to rise into a slight wind, and we pendulumed up the first ten feet. I grabbed one side as she stumbled back and forth.

Well that's no fun, she said. A man with spiked blond hair began running toward us from a circus tent, shouting.

Let's fix that, she said, and fired up the gas.

We shot up a hundred feet in a second; my stomach dropped, my ears popped, the gas roared.

Down below a crowd had gathered where we'd been just a minute before, clumped together in the trampled grass as if they'd emptied into a drain. They were all waving. I peered over and waved back.

Now they started with both hands.

I glanced at my companion. She smiled at me, but something looked wrong with her eyes. Her eyelids seemed filled with fluid, as if she'd just been stung by a hundred bees.

Are you drunk? I asked.

She slipped her lower lip over her upper one and seemed to consider the question. We were still going up, moving laterally as well, and below us, the people were just dots. I could still make out the funeral home with the cars around it and then it too slipped into other buildings, a river entering the sea. The pleasant scent of manure came from distant fields.

Define drunk, she said at last, shouting over the roar of the burning gas.

We climbed so quickly. The sudden chill raised goosebumps on my arms, the sky deepened into indigo, a weird green phosphorescence trembled around the balloon.

Have you done this before? I asked.

She smiled and nodded. Her eyes were the same startling cornflower blue as my mother's. Oh yes, she said. Of course. Once. But that time someone else was in control. She leaned back in the corner and slid down, letting her head fall against her knees and, in a movement of peculiar modesty, tented her blouse away from her chest and threw up inside it.

The numbers on my watch were just visible. The visitation was almost over. Soon everyone would file out and look up at the sky, to find balloons glowing like immature stars, not quite ready to take their spot in the heavens. Higher up, if they tilted their heads a bit more, they might see us rising and rising, a speck of light streaking across the Milky Way. They'd think of my mother, I hoped, beginning her immense journey, and for the moment I was glad.

Once the fuel ran out—I imagined darkness, the crippling cold, a furious plummeting, perhaps what my mother had felt at the end—I expected a different reaction.

Open Season

The morning headline said the season had just opened, which of course we knew; I'd paid for my permit and stored my clothes overnight in a dry-cleaning bag filled with sweaty T-shirts, a box of doughnuts and some bus exhaust, not easy to come by but absolutely crucial if I didn't want to spook my prey. And I was sure Juan had done something similar and then indulged in one of his many superstitions, perhaps putting on his right sock and shoe before touching his left ones, or wearing his yellow under-shirt, or scribbling on his tongue with pens until he could taste the ink. Most of the people in Hopping John's diner probably had too, though few would care to admit it. The hunting gene ran deep, even if over the years a lot of people had grown wary of it, or ashamed.

The place was loud, we had a long day in front of us, we'd already paid. Juan sighed, crossed his knife and fork on the plate, shoved the plate aside and drummed his fingers on the newspa-per, which lay folded open on the counter next to his coffee mug. One headline concerned the shortened length of the season, another hoarding and a secret government cabal; when Juan's fingers stopped drumming, I looked at his newly still hands. When he made a clucking noise with his tongue like a bat hitting a ball, sweat prickled my armpits; he was up to something, and I was suddenly afraid that he was going to win our bet.

Yankees, he said, though he said it with the wrong accent— *Yahn-keys* rather than *Yank-ease*—so he didn't get the word.

Pretty cheap way to bag your first one of the season, but he'd started it, drawing out the word and failing to capture it, so I said *Yankees* the correct way and when the word floated free, expanding to full size in midair, I grabbed it. *What a word*, I thought, balancing its heavy weight in my palm, sniffing it, finding it as fragrant as a ripe melon. Automatically I began field-dressing the little bugger, slitting it from anus to breast-bone while taking care not to pierce the stomach—not wanting to lose my own breakfast from the smell—and finally reaching two fingers up into the chest cavity to grab hold of the wind-pipe and yank it loose. My game bag was in the car so I asked the waitress for some wax paper and foil. She came back with them and our change just as I scooped out the intestines, and I felt Juan looking at the waitress looking at me, or rather, at the steaming entrails piled on my plate like a bag of eels. Her face had turned a pistachio green.

Sorry, I said. Thought you'd seen it before.

I have, she said at last and looked up. It's just, I don't know, first day of the season, you know? Every year, it still surprises me.

I tore off the newspaper's front page. The headline said that the Word Institute was declaring a shortage; the subheadings noted the danger of words going extinct and that the government might start revoking licenses next year, but Juan and I didn't believe it. There were plenty of words around, if you knew where to look. I made a neat packet of the newspaper and the wax paper and folded the foil around both, careful not to bend the *Y* or get pricked by the pointed ends of the *K*. Captured, emptied of entrails, the word made a nice small package.

You going to keep that with you all day? Juan said.

Have to, I said, tucking it inside my jacket pocket. What else is there to do?

He shrugged, swept the change into his cupped palm, and dropped a few bills on the counter. I don't know, he said, his voice flat. It's going to smell by the end of the day.

I knew he was feeling anxious and depressed; it seems like everyone else gets theirs first and you'll never get yours. I left a few extra bills to make up for upsetting the waitress, slipped off my stool and patted his shoulder.

Relax, Juan, I said. It's an Anglo newspaper. Back in the Dominican, the word would have been yours.

Which was true. Even so, when I went into the restroom to wash the ink off my shaking hands, I found myself grinning at my reflection. I'd lain awake most of the night before, trembling in anticipation and worried about our bet, and then burst out sweating when Juan made the first move. Now I rinsed my face with cold water, drawing my skin tight and letting the moment linger.

Sometimes it felt like you needed a mallet and a cold chisel to free the words, and then others were just *there*, shimmering. You could almost smell them on the air, like coming rain. It didn't matter if it was the season or not, though neither Juan nor I had any patience for poaching, the punishments for which were justly swift and extreme. Home confinement, loss of hunting privileges. Juan and I were professionals. People, I think, envied us. I know I had, younger. The skills, the knowledge, the almost talismanic air that hung about the best word hunters.

I'd had their trading cards, thin portraits with pictures and stats, the cards smelling of the accompanying thick sticks of gum, pink like a pressed tongue. Men but not men—lords, almost gods. I ran my fingers over their names and spoke them aloud, repeating them until they became words rather than names, repeating them so often they became finally not even words but sensations on my tongue and teeth, lips and palate, a kind of click and hum that spread through muscle and bone to blood and veins, circulating throughout my body so that I throbbed with it, asleep and awake.

I felt myself humming now, with my first word bagged on the first day of the season and words all around me, hidden but incipient. The words were feeling the pull too, wanting almost to come out, to seek that which sought them, capture as a form of release. The joining of them and us that seemed both ordained and inevitable and that stretched back in time to before time's beginning, to before there was firmament and sea, daylight and night, language and humanity. To when there was only darkness and void, and then there was the word. We felt that, Juan and I and his wife Katerina and all the other hunters, and the words felt it too, sensed it, lived trembling with that awesome knowledge, the mystic cords of memory that bound us. Or so we liked to say when we'd been drinking and were full of romantic notions.

But best of all? Right now, I was in the lead.

Most of our younger colleagues were sticking close to the city, trying to put themselves in places where words often gather, like magazine stands, advertising agencies, lawyers' offices—but Juan and I were airily dismissive of these tactics. First, if you did find words there, it was usually the easy, immature ones, never more than a single syllable and often only articles (which in many states aren't even legal game), and second, it just isn't likely to happen. Young hunters never realize how smart mature words are, or how difficult hunting them can be: you can't glass a field for them, you can't float-hunt them, they give off no scent and leave no form, if they survive long enough to grow into multisyllabics, they know when the season's about to begin. And a lot of new hunters are so raw they even believe the lies about old Indian words lurking on the riverbanks. It's a great tradition to send newbies after them, like having rookies fetch bags of steam from the trainer.

Thinking this made me a little abashed to have grabbed the year's first word from a newspaper—I mean, how obvious can you be?—and I guessed Juan was feeling the same when he suggested we drive out to the Rotary Lodge.

I also suspected he was still peeved that I'd beaten him to the punch, and maybe this was his way of working that off, of restoring his luck—we hadn't seen a single copy of *Fowler's Modern English Usage* yet, after all, and maybe at the lodge we would—so I said fine. I should have known better. He's just too good to be sloppy. Nonetheless, all the way out, I found myself thinking of that field of lavender, my chances at being able to harvest it for good.

Lavender was a word I'd loved since childhood, the first I remember: its look on the page, its sound in the ear, its scent on the air. Even its feel in the mouth, how, speaking it, the tongue darts forward, slides back to the palate, and finally retreats toward the throat. La-ven-der. One of the few words to get the tongue to do that.

Juan and I had planted the field back when I was married in hopes that the word would show up, natural habitat and all, though so far it hadn't happened. Would the third time be a lucky charm? Last year when we'd gone we'd found nothing. No words, that is. Not *heat*, though it was hot; not *bees*, though there were thousands. Juan had been stung but gamely stuck it out; he must have known I was up to something. We'd bet, finally, that whoever bagged the most words this season would earn rights to the lavender for life.

This year the crop hadn't flourished, because neither my wife nor I had tended it after our divorce. Hunting, she'd said, when she'd told me of her plans to leave. If I were a word, maybe you'd pay half as much attention to me. I didn't think it would be good form to tell her she was right.

Now I was hoping to win again and find a way to tend the field too, maybe sell some of what I caught. After all, what color word could be better than *lavender*? Three syllables, even.

Aquamarine, I suppose, but I'd never liked the sound of that one, finding it harsh, and others of equal value—*burnt umber* and *cadmium*—were ugly to see and to say. To me, of course. To someone else, to Juan, even, they might be breathtaking.

In the divorce my wife got the house and I the field, or at least harvesting rights to it. She also got most of my words, which I knew she was selling; I'd seen them, stuffed and mounted, on eBay. It killed me, but I wouldn't stoop to buying them back. It had taken years to build that collection and now it would take years more, but I told myself that that was all right. I was still relatively young and the day had started off really well; maybe *lavender* was in my future.

I recognized the Rotary Lodge when we got there. In April they had hosted a Spanish Scrabble tournament, but it turned out the real reason Juan wanted to go back was the Kentucky Wildcat flag fluttering on the flagpole. As soon as he got out of the car he locked onto it—I saw it too, but he'd brought us here so I couldn't say a thing. Normally, he was the stillest hunter I knew, and here he'd gone beyond stillness to bliss; his whole body was trembling. I spotted the food plot, the salt lick, the feeders.

When did you pick up on their routines? I said, and wondered if he'd set up a mock-scrape on one of our earlier visits without my noticing.

Not 'their,' he said. Just the short one.

Blue? I started to say, but as my lips formed the word I choked it off and he laughed.

Yes, he said, *Blue*, and cradled it in his hands once it dropped from the flag. It looked as light as cotton candy. Right after, he said *Wildcat*, which appeared heavier, but before saying the last word he waited. Why not? It was a big moment. He'd come in hopes of finding a single small word and had stumbled across

three, two of which were multis. Overhead, a plane glinted in
the sun as it made a long slow curve to the east and the warm
west wind carried the silty scent of the river to us. He closed
his eyes and breathed in deeply before saying *Kentucky*, then
opened his eyes to watch it come to him.

Three words at once, and a rare one, two, three-syllable tri-
fecta at that; it was so good I couldn't even feel jealous. Instead,
I allowed him the pleasure of field dressing all three of them.
He was so happy that before he gutted them, he let me have
first dibs smelling *Kentucky*. Is fawn a scent? It seemed so. Next
came tobacco, rich and ruddy, followed by mint and fresh-cut
grass and something swampy; I had to sit a minute to clear my
head. After, I squatted and watched him work on *Blue*, which
seemed surprisingly sticky, almost tarry, so much so he had to
stop repeatedly to wipe his hands on the grass.

Like all good hunters, he avoided the tarsal glands, but we
did have our differences. He cut through a few ribs before reaching up into the chest, a step I usually found unnecessary, and he
only removed half the diaphragm before cleaning out the lower
organs. Then again, his clearing of the esophagus, heart, and
lungs was one elegant motion, though I found myself ignoring
that because *Blue*'s ink was black.

Is that common? I asked.

Never heard of it, he said.

Do you think it's sick?

Could be. Something this small, we won't eat it anyway.

That made sense. When he started on *Kentucky* I lit a
cigarette.

Sure you want to do that? Juan asked as he hacked his way
through an especially stubborn breastbone.

I don't believe the research, I said.

He finished the breastbone in silence and emptied out the
organs, propped open the body cavity with a stick. I found the
hose and turned it on. He began rinsing out the bladder area.

Well, he said, for what it's worth, I don't either.

The Word Institute had recently published a paper about words being spooked by smoke, but years of hunting lore and our own experiences told a different story.

When the water ran clear I turned it off and we both stood over the cleaned words, admiring them; they were still fresh enough not to have lost their shape, though it was warm and they soon would. They were just beginning to pale.

Here, I said, step aside. I snapped a bunch of pictures with my phone camera, first of the words by themselves and next of Juan holding them in various combinations, and texted the photos to his wife as a surprise; she was going to be really happy for him. *Kentucky* is rare up north, and it was going to push him past halfway on his states; *Blue* completed his color wheel, which she'd accomplished the year before. *Wildcat* was just plain fun. I couldn't remember ever seeing Juan look so pleased.

Still, he joked about his luck, an act some of our younger colleagues fell for, but Juan's always been a serious hunter. Years ago he replaced four molars with type keys from the city's afternoon papers after they shut down. We'd gone to check out the press's former site, soon to be a sponge factory, the buildings long since demolished, and he was scuffing at the bricky dirt with his heel, turning up chunks of type keys with triumph.

Sixty-eight years they printed the paper here, he said, squatting as he bagged the stuff. Sixty-eight years.

His hands shook as he handed me three letters. *H, T, R.* Think of it, he said, and closed my fingers around them. Each of these helped stamp out thousands of words. He was so intense that his reverence was catching, and I keep the type keys now in my bedside table, fingering them blindly nights I can't sleep.

He must have hauled forty pounds of the stuff out of the ground, which he took home and soaked in type wash. Which ones he implanted I don't know; I've asked, but he won't tell me, even drunk, even late, even bragging about bringing down the elusive clause. Superstitions run deep. Supposedly the dishwasher at Hopping John's was once a lawyer with veneers implanted on his eyeteeth, but then he drank too much at one Christmas office party, flicked on the building-wide intercom and announced their contents (*miasma* or *refulgent*, the story differs). Since then, he's been as luckless as a carwash. I've never believed it, but we all have our cautionary tales.

Lunch was a bust. I kept thinking I saw things: in the menu (too obvious), on the clotted surface of my chowder (a long blond hair), in the nondairy coffee creamer (the sheen of oil). Nothing, though. After lunch, we parked the car in a city lot, stuffed folded-up bills into the proper pay slot and hopped a bus for downtown, which was so crowded we were like a box of nails. A few of the riders had those obnoxious new ringtones, made from Hitler's speeches. They all seemed to go off at once, and I ignored them, though Juan couldn't. His face darkened and I shook my head at him, silently urging him to let it go, but he ignored me.

The bus was slow. For a couple of miles we swayed silently against the other passengers—most of whom tried to give us room because we smelled of ink, bitter and enticing, though I noticed a few surreptitiously admiring glances, especially from those reading their dog-eared English grammars—until Juan caught me staring.

Jesus, he said, switching handholds on the hanging strap as he switched to Spanish. You don't have to be so blatant.

No importa, I said, switching to Spanish myself. I'm a mountaineer. I've climbed peaks like that before.

Yet the truth was I was stalling; I'd frozen. It doesn't happen often, maybe once every three or four years, but I'm staring at a word and can't say it. Some kind of mechanical breakdown, I think: I recognize the word as a word, but I can't remember how

it sounds, its shape in my mouth, and so I have to wait and hope
no one else sees it in the meantime, all the while forming different words with my teeth and tongue, trying to recall it. I try not
to look like a pointer pointing at its prey, but Juan knows me
too well for me to cover up. He probably didn't get it this time
because he was still floating from his triple.

The word was right there in front of me, tucked into a woman's cleavage, trying to blend in with a crescent of tiny freckles
and the sheen of sweat. Natural habitat, and all that; very smart,
as multis usually are. When I glanced away to read an advertising placard about elocution lessons it came to me. *Silicone*, I
said, and it was mine.

Happens to me every year, the woman said.

I hadn't expected her to speak and her voice surprised me,
higher than I'd have guessed, less polished. You'd think I'd be
used to it, she said, which told me that she wasn't, and for the
first time in a long time I was embarrassed. For me, not her.
In my linguistic lust I hadn't thought of her as a person or
her breasts as breasts, but that's probably not how it appeared
to her—early-season words are generally focused more on sex
than food, after all—and I noticed her then, really looked at
her, the bias-cut brunette hair, the pretty oval face, the silver
rope necklace just touching a single mole on her left collar-
bone, the faint pink flush rising from beneath her pale skin like
red ink diffusing in water, uniting her freckles in a single cinnamon landscape.

I wished we could start over again, I wished I could ask her
out, I wished I could ask her why she didn't hunt, especially
since she knew it would happen every year, but you couldn't
ask that, any more than you'd ask a stranger about their favorite
sexual position. People's feelings about hunting were complex,
complicated now by the apparent sudden decline in available
words. As they became scarcer (the Word Institute had all kinds
of theories as to why), jobs and hunting licenses were becoming

scarcer too. But perhaps her mood had nothing to do with that; perhaps she was just sad to lose a word.

I stammered out an apology and gestured that I could put the word back, but she raised her eyebrows and opened her eyes wide and tilted her head as if to say, Really? Which made me feel worse and ended any idea of romance, so I was left with only two options: dropping the word or proceeding as normal. I'd have liked to have done the first, but I was already behind in my bet to Juan and even if I did drop it, someone else would simply grab it, so, blushing myself, I stretched the word out on the floor and squatted over it and brought out my knife.

Like all silicones, it was slippery and I had to use one foot to keep it pinned. I'd have liked to sniff it before gutting, but with the woman watching there was no way I was going to. Who knew what she'd think of me then? Still, I could imagine it, the plastic scent of water from a hose, sweat, her jasmine perfume, a zested orange. One *silicone* had smelled like that and it had always stuck with me. Now, though, I had work to do.

The bus swerved; we all nearly toppled onto the sitters, and when it hit three potholes in a row, we groaned. Juan was glaring at the driver.

The driver can't tell you're mad at him, I said. He probably can't even see you in the mirror.

I got on with it, the first gush of fragrant ink squirting across the runneled rubber floor, making it shine, and three drops splashing on the woman's left ankle. They hung there, quivering, and it took all my will power to keep from wiping them off with my thumb. I hoped she'd notice my restraint and think more kindly of me, but when I looked up she was looking away. My chivalry had gone unnoticed.

Then Juan dropped his bomb. *Pop-ups*, he said, and there they were, four of them on the windshield. I couldn't believe it. The prick of a driver had been driving while looking at his phone. Juan bagged three of them but someone sitting just

behind the driver poached the fourth. I couldn't see her, as I
had my head down, concentrating on my labor, though I heard
her gravelly voice as she said *Flibbertigibbet*. *Quite a catch*, I
thought, *two syllables better than mine, and without the awkward
social embarrassment too.*

Even without those five syllables Juan had me. We were through
hunting in the city and back in the parking lot where we'd
dropped our car, about to head home. The lot was already half-
empty, the sky darkening, passing cars were flipping on their
headlights. A few had words strapped to their roofs. Not yet
gutted, they took up a lot of room. It wasn't a sight we were
going to see much more of; within a week of the season's start,
most of the big words will have gone nocturnal.

Juan's bag was fattened with Spanish words. Mine too.
Intermediate Spanish; my accent is good enough, my vocab-
ulary pretty large. It only makes sense, since more and more
of them are moving into the area, but no matter how much
I study I'll never be able to catch some, especially those with
voiced dental fricatives; my tongue just can't do certain things.
Still, I try. Years ago, after he brought down *Atascadero*, liking
its rhythm and pulse, I recorded Juan saying it on my phone,
followed by a whole string of words at once, a nonsense poem
he made up on the spot, *pan, piedra, el final del camino*, just to
help refine my ear and train my tongue. Now I roll my *r*'s like
tumbleweed.

We were beat, and it was clear that Juan had won. Though I
never like to lose, I've worked really hard at being gracious, so I
was on the point of sticking out my hand when something about
the two guys lingering at the corner caught my eye. Maybe it
was a flash of light on the mailbox from a turning car.

They were in suits, trying to look casual.

I steered us a little closer, asked one for a cigarette. He patted his pockets, touching each repeatedly with both flat palms, like a baseball manager giving signs, smiled, said he was all out. His buddy didn't even look my way. Sunglasses at dusk, and they both smelled like olive oil.

Did you guys work on the phone booths too? I asked.

Juan had no idea what I was talking about, but their heads snapped around and I knew I had them. I'd read about it, how the government was removing mailboxes. A certain number in the city had disappeared, just as the phone booths had. It was supposed to be quiet—they didn't identify targets ahead of time, as a way of avoiding protests—but rumor was they were collecting the mailboxes and destroying the words. I pictured the whole thing, how they'd swerve close, grab the mailbox and bundle it into their van, speed to the local airport on the edge of town when they had enough, take the helicopter ride over the ocean, throw open the side door and hold on against the rotor wash as they tipped box after box out into the black air. They'd be so far up they wouldn't even hear the splash.

I asked, Are you Special Services?

They didn't even look at one another before saying, in unison, We can neither confirm nor deny that.

Special Ops, I said, and then, quickly, *Special Operations*, and all the words leaked out of the mail slot, followed by others, cascading to the pavement like a jackpot.

Both Juan and I were speechless, though Juan recovered far more quickly than I. He didn't even wait. He shook my hand, said I had him, asked how soon I'd get them mounted. The only bad moment came when he raised his phone to take a picture and they knocked it out of his hands.

No photos, they said. They asked to see our hunting licenses before agreeing that the words were ours. A mere formality; even Special Ops guys have to bow to the power of law, or at least to this one. After we flashed our licenses they left, crushing Juan's phone underfoot to be sure we got the message.

I don't know, I said, finally answering Juan. The words were
right there, puddled at my feet, and one of them, tucked under
a couple of others, I spent a long time looking at. *Holy shit*,
I thought, *there it is. Lavender*. I pictured the brilliant scented
field, swaying in the hot summer wind, tasted the word in my
mouth, smelled it. Juan knew of my fascination, though I'd
never spoken of it.

All I had to do was pick it up, pick *them* up, but my hands
were shaking so badly I didn't trust them. I knew where I was
going to mount the words, a patch in my living room over the
fireplace I'd left bare on purpose (aside from the swatches of
wallpaper I used to hunt as a boy), the kind of space every hunter
has for that perfect trophy. I even had the spotlight in my base-
ment, ready to mount above them. And yes, because it was *lavender*, the light would be too. Form follows function, and all that.

But even as my hands began to still I couldn't bring myself
to reach down for the words, and at first, I couldn't figure out
what was wrong. I mean, *lavender* was my holy grail. And who
among us isn't fascinated by the black ops, the interplay of language and death? This one to live, that one to die.

Once I'd captured the word *please*. I'd heard it in my mind,
just before slicing it open. Please! it seemed to say, which was
unnerving, though it hadn't stopped me, and its guts had been
as hot and as sticky as any other's, its ink as blue. I still thought
about it at odd times, dreamed of it, sometimes after leafing
through *The Word Hunter's Bible* and letting its table of contents
run across the back of my closed eyelids. Field Care of Words,
Home Care of Words, Word-hunting Hazards. The very chapters I'd read last night, though I hadn't heard the word then, so
I didn't know why it came to me again now. *Please*. This time I
listened, finding it strange; at first there was nothing, and then
there was the word.

And listening to it changed *lavender* for me. There on the
ground, surrounded by *special ops* and all the other words

the mailbox had so surprisingly disgorged, *lavender* seemed unscented and curiously pale, nothing like what I'd expected. My response was visceral and overpowering; I wanted nothing to do with it. Juan seemed to understand. He stood so close our shoes were touching, and the smell of the ink on his hands—a little more acrid than mine, a little richer—was overpowering. Mixed feelings? he said.

It was all I could do to nod. I was thinking that the phone booths were one thing, with their graffiti and scratched-in names and, very rarely, a phonebook, but the mailboxes were something else entirely. By law, the Special Ops guys were supposed to empty them before dropping them into the sea, but they'd been granted immunity from prosecution in case they didn't (it was likely they'd miss one or two letters in night ops, after all, and the argument was that they really shouldn't be held accountable for that) and no one had the authority to check on them. The thought of all those letters dropping to their doom, all those wasted words, was just too chilling to contemplate; it was terrifying to imagine the sounds those words made, struggling to articulate themselves before it was too late, their searing echoes bouncing around inside that plunging dark metal box. It made me ashamed of my country. Years ago, young and green, we wouldn't have let that happen.

My hands felt slick and I just couldn't do it.

It's all right, Juan said, patting me on my back. If we walk away, someone else will come across them. They won't go to waste. I promise you. Without context, the words will be free of taint. His voice had that soft Spanish burr I've always admired.

And that helped me. I knew he was right, that someone else would take them, maybe a homeless woman who could trade them for something useful. Food, fire, a pen to write her own words with, a hunting blind to sit in and watch other words flock to her words in order to hide. After all, who would think to hunt words inside a hunting blind?

At least that's what I told myself on the long ride home, which, when I got there, was completely dark. I left it that way, maneuvering by touch, slipping both *Yankees* and *silicone* into the freezer with averted eyes. I should have soaked them in ice water to age them before they were frozen, if I really wanted them to last, those and the Spanish words stuffed into my bag, but at the moment I just didn't care. Instead, I felt along the wall like a blind man to the hallway opening and stumbled out to my favorite living-room chair, where I sat in the dark for a long time, facing the dark empty fireplace and the slightly paler empty space above it, telling myself that my hands resting on my knees looked black because I had no lights on, because I was growing older and my eyes were weakening, and not because they were covered with ink. *Please.* Oh, I wanted to believe it. And as I stared at my hands in the enveloping darkness, I almost did.

Rock, Paper, Scissors

I'm leaning over the construction fence watching a concrete saw throw off twin fans of sparks and mud—it's water-cooled—impressed that the guy's freehanding a line as straight as a level, when Tommy slaps my helmet with the blueprints and says, Get your ass in gear.

Cover's up, so I slip down first, carrying bags of tools and both our lunchboxes.

He clanks down after me and clicks on his headlamp, lighting up a graffiti tag. Maize and blue, a Michigan fan. Tommy smacks it with his wrench. Asshat, he says, and I know what kind of day I'm in for; other times, they're just overly rambunctious kids, stupidly misguided and adventurous, but today they're on the outs. The world will be too, which includes me. Some days I can get him out of it, work him like Play-Doh, but today doesn't feel like that day.

Before we leave the funnel of light, he thumbs his walkie-talkie, Rogers it, and says, Rain today, like I didn't know. Above us, the sky is a swollen silver balloon.

Heavy, he says. Keep your ears open.

Like I won't. I wait for Tommy to say, Don't leave anything lying around, which he always does. Instead he turns and says, You put us behind on Friday already. Let's move.

I didn't put us behind, I say. It was an emergency repair. You know that.

Yeah. And I also know if you hadn't argued, it'd have been done faster. Now let's go. He squats and pushes ahead, big shoulders jamming up the tunnel.

A pipe had split; we could repair it with a slip-liner or by curing, and I'd held out for curing. We had a UV generator with us to check electrical insulation anyway—corona discharge—and the fit would be tighter, a real seal, but Tommy thought we could get a slip-liner faster than a resin-impregnated one.

I squat and crabwalk after him, wondering why he's bringing it up again. I'd won in the end, since if we'd used a slip-liner we might have to repair it another time later, and it hadn't seemed to bother him then. But maybe it was Friday's dinner, when I'd had a weirdly erotic run-in with his wife. I hope to God it's not.

We stand, and instead of yelling back, guilt makes me try another route: being solicitous. Watch your head up there at the corner, I say. Low pipes.

I'm not a fucking moron, he says, and speeds up, safety helmet knocking against the pipe. His neck snaps back but he doesn't stop.

Jesus, I think, *he's going to kill himself just to prove it*, and I know it's not a bee he's got up his ass, it's an entire colony.

Our clanking tools echo off the walls. Overhead we hear footsteps and murmured conversations—the tunnel's just below the surface here—which combines with the smell of dirt to make it seem like we're dead and the living are going on without us. I don't say anything about it; the mood Tommy's in, he'd ride me about that too. Then all hell breaks loose—a herd of buffalo stampeding above us—which passes just as quickly as it came.

Christ, Tommy says, and stops, letting me go ahead. What rain.

I turn the next corner and light up a skull hanging from a steampipe; in the flashlight the eye sockets look as deep as forever.

What's got you spooked now? Tommy says, shouldering by me, and though his voice doesn't sound into it, I know he set it up. Friday afternoon—the thirteenth, of course—he was gone a bit, and we were scheduled to come this way until the pipe broke.

The plaster of Paris crumbles when I touch it. That's good, I say. Took some effort. Props, bro.

It wasn't me, he says. Must have been some other asshole.

Some *other* asshole? I say, hoping humor might crack his crust. You saying you're one too?

He turns, comes back, gets right in my face. Quit screwing around, he says, breath smelling of coffee. Let's just get this done.

I start marking down things for future repairs—a grate that some urbexers must have broken through, and a turbine with a bent blade—thinking, *It's got to be Donna. But how on earth could he know?*

The whole thing started out innocently enough, with her telling me about a trip with her nieces and nephews to Chuck E. Cheese's. In the tube maze, she said, she was moving slow, and one of the kids behind her pushed her butt and told her to go faster.

She said, I mean, I know it's a big target, but come on!

She hadn't been flirting, I knew that, but all during dinner I couldn't help thinking about that ass, though I didn't feel it was obvious; even my date hadn't noticed. But I wonder now if my disloyal thoughts hadn't been shining from my skin like ice.

The turbine's bent blade I rate a priority two, and Tommy looks at it, shakes his head.

Too fucking low, he says. Get your head out of your ass.

Why? I say. To look at you? I prefer to keep it there.

No shit, he says. You always have. Tunnels have to be continuously functional, he says, as if I'm worse than a newbie, a noob. It's a three.

No way, I say. The grate's a three. More people get in here, they can screw up the steam pipes and the tunnel gets compromised.

If steam was going to escape, it already would have. Mark it a three.

Technically, he's my boss, but he's never told me what to do, not like this. Something else is going on here, and though I want to tell him to give it a rest I let it go because I don't know what it is, and add an extra curve to the number.

My acquiescence seems to make him angrier. Now that wasn't so hard, was it? he says. For once in your life, you listened.

We pass through a factory steam tunnel, a bad old one with roaches and rats, built poorly and maintained worse. Hot—120, easily—with an awkward system requiring separate air vents subject to waterhammer, and while I'm crawling beneath the pipes, pushing the lunchboxes before me and dragging the tool bag with my ankle, they start banging like someone's slamming them with a sledge. Near the end a steamflash spurts from one of the fittings and I hold up the lunchboxes to shield my face.

Tommy's there, pale as someone who's passed in the tunnel's dead light, wiping off his coveralls. Take enough time? he says. I could have had my fucking lunch already.

No, you couldn't, I say, and stand. I'm carrying it, remember?

He shakes his head, but before he can say anything his walkie-talkie squawks like it's being attacked, though neither of us can make out what's being said. No texts come through either; too much static, too many pipes, this far underground. I click mine off and we go on. I stumble and bump into Tommy, because the ground beneath my boot seems buckled, and he says, Can't you be serious for once?

I scuff at where I tripped, find nothing, start up again, and soon it's like we've entered a mall; though we're the deepest we've been, this tunnel has high ceilings, fluorescent lights, dry air. Graffiti too, of course, and I read the tags using the trick Donna taught me: just go by the tops of the letters, which usually make sense.

Tommy spreads out the blueprints and I push aside thoughts of his wife, poke at a door marked near where we're standing, say, Why didn't we just enter there?

That's why we're here in the first place. Rebuilding something there and they have to dig. Want to make sure it hasn't damaged the steam system.

He flips through the blueprints, past the page where we are to ones of the offices above, and puts one fat finger on a drawing. That's where Donna works, he says.

So it is Donna, I think, yet maybe it isn't me, watching him study the plans as if he could see her in her cubicle. At last he breathes in deeply, rolls them up, and tells me to get going; we've each got our steam table calculator and making sure the steam traps are purging condensate won't be hard, though it will take time.

I start at the far end, glad we're working apart, since it lets my anger recede and my mind wander to Donna. Friday, toward the end of dinner, she'd asked Tommy to dance.

You know I don't dance, he said. Truth was, I'd never seen her dance either.

How about you? she said, looking at me. Brianna's hand tensed on my thigh, but I was feeling happy and still thinking about her butt, so I said, Sure, and we headed out to the floor.

Halfway there the band switched to a salsa number, but I refused to chicken out, though in the end I moved about as well as if I'd been marching in mud. Donna, short and dark, turned out to be as flexible as an eel.

I'm lost in those thoughts when Tommy calls out to me.

How many have you done?

I tell him.

Four? His echoing voice brims with disgust, sounding like I've disappointed an entire crowd. He tells me how many he's done.

Six? I say, not adding what I think: done that quickly means they weren't done right.

He says, Get to work and quit jerkin' your gherkin.

My face flushes, and I'm glad he can't see me. If he only knew how I'd spent my weekend.

We work. Noises bubble up from underfoot, which doesn't make sense. One time I think it's voices, another footsteps; the last time sounds like a distant choir. While I'm trying to figure it out Tommy asks how many more I've done. I've sped up a bit and he's slowed down by the same amount, since we've each serviced three more.

Sixteen out of twenty-four, he says. Not bad. We've broken the back of it, let's break for lunch.

It's how we roll: work hard steady and fast early on, then relax for the last part of the shift, and I've always liked it. Other crews cruise until near the end, then hurry everything up, but that's when you make mistakes. Closing things up takes time.

I give him his lunchbox and he squats over it, resting his hand on it for so long you'd think his death certificate was inside, then flips it open. A black-and-orange Reese's Cup wrapper pops into view.

Donna left you, I say without thinking, and Tommy gives me the finger. But I know it's true. For three years he's always had cookies or brownies, and extra for me. She wouldn't send him off like that unless she was sick, and if she was sick he'd have told me.

I say, What happened?

Fuck if I know.

God, that's horrible. You two seemed so good.

Tell me about it. Out of the blue. We came home from dinner and fought.

The dancing? I say, before I can stop myself.

He looks up, puzzled. What? No. His eyes flick back down. The wine.

The wine, I think. Then, *I'd have left you too.*

At O'Callahan's, when the waitress asked if we wanted drinks, Donna had said, You have a wine list?

First time I'd heard her ask that. Must have been for Tommy too. Wine? he said. Like you know about wine.

He'd had a few, but still. Donna's face always showed everything, and now it was a mixture of hurt and shame.

Hey, I said, trying to salvage the night. She knows more about it than me.

So would a bag of lightbulbs, he said. We'll have a pitcher of Bud.

Donna picked up the triangular Specials advertiser in the center of the table and turned it in her hands. I don't know, she said. I just wanted to try something different.

Different? He shook his head. Do the math. Even with those prices, it would cost more than the beer.

I wasn't thinking about dollars and ounces.

You should. After two, you wouldn't taste it anyway.

Yeah, Brianna said, trying to be helpful. Fun's better when it's cheap.

It deteriorated from there, with Donna dissing Tommy's order and Tommy asking if she was on the rag. But when the food was done Donna seemed to rally, which was when she asked about dancing.

I came back to the table sweating and grinning.

She can really move, I said.

So I noticed, Tommy said. Brianna didn't say a thing to me, and I knew the night was over. Whatever storm was coming would probably be better for Donna if we weren't there, so I made our excuses, dropped fifty on the table, and left. Brianna and I had it out before we even got to the car and hadn't talked since, but I didn't know about Tommy and Donna. Now, I can guess.

He's squatting, staring at the two perfect rectangles of his sandwich; Donna always cut them diagonally. Then he unwraps the Reese's and pops them both in, crumples the wrapper and throws it aside, pats the sandwich, stacks the halves, squares them up, and rewraps them tightly. They disappear into his lunchbox with a click.

I don't know, he says and stands, I'm not hungry today.

Me either, I say, which isn't true—I'm suddenly starving—but I play along. We can save it for break.

Must be that steam we passed through, he says. All I want to do is sleep.

I'll bet. It must be driving you nuts. I mean, God. One day you got a wife, the next day you don't. I'm sorry.

But the thing is, I realize I'm not and that I'm saying this—ostensibly to make him feel better—only to make him feel worse. I wonder, *Where did that come from*, this harping on it, this desire not to let him forget?

I reach for the Reese's wrapper.

Leave it, he says, and I understand: angry, he wants everything to go to hell. After all, what have all his rules gotten him? Never cheated on his wife, never missed a day of work, never took shortcuts on the job. He's taught me almost everything I know, and for that reason I'm not going to help him out. Sooner or later he'll have to come back to his normal meticulous self, and the less far that journey is, the better. And don't I feel good for thinking so.

I pick the wrapper up and it's sticky, coated in melted chocolate, and I remember holding the lunchboxes up against the steam. I try to shake it free from my palm, can't, the melted chocolate like glue.

Water's seeping out from beneath the sealed door, and, very faintly, it sounds like someone's knocking against it from the other side. I squat, put my palm in the water to clean it, ask, That hospital dig, is it near water?

What?

There's water leaking from under the door.

His face pales. Water?

That's what I said.

Water? he says, so still he might have been replaced by a statue. Get up and get out, now.

His lunchbox hits the ground before I realize what he means, then I'm running too, ditching the lunchbox and tool bag, unhitching utility belts as I run, blood so loud in my ears I don't even hear them hit.

I pass him—all those years of Donna's lasagnas and meat pies—then get to the steam tunnel, where he pauses, winded.

I stop, say, Come on.

Go, he says, bent over and heaving, hands on his knees. He picks one up and waves weakly. I'll be there.

I get behind him and push. Go, fucker. I ain't stopping again.

He starts crawling and, before he's halfway through, my palms and knees are suddenly wet and the water murmuring behind us, and then it's sloshing at our thighs and forearms. How the hell does it rise so fast?

Tommy's standing again, feet splashing as he runs, and I'm after him, water at my calves, trip over the broken grate, sprawl,

slide into the sidewall. I scramble to my feet and we go on. The
opening of the smaller tunnel ahead grows even smaller as we
get closer and Tommy throws himself into it headfirst and I follow after, the water cold and dirty, swirling at my crotch and
stomach, pushing against me. I yell, Go faster, or think I do,
but Tommy must be moving as fast as he can. I'm jammed up
against him and feel like I'm sinking, like the water is hunting
me down. The worst moment is when I realize it is.

Twenty yards, I think, I'm not going to make it, and I'm
right: the water's at my face. I jerk back, hit my head on the
steam pipes, stop on all fours, close my eyes, close my mouth,
fist my hands and make myself scramble on, and then the water
pushes me forward and pops me out, slamming me into Tommy,
who helps me stand.

But only for a second before a wall of water knocks us down
and we surge past the opening, jam our feet against the sides,
push back as the raging water tries to spin us around; I throw
my hand up, grab the rung, start climbing while sucking air.

Two rungs up I reach down for him. His hand goes for mine
and then he's staring at my palm. Grab it! I scream, but he just
pulls his hand down, looks at me, tucks his arms to his sides and
disappears.

Oh God, I think, and climb down until the water surges up
around my waist when, terrified, I'm climbing so fast I shoot out
onto the rainy pavement like I'm at the head of a geyser, which
I am; the water spills out around me, pushing up Tommy's yellow helmet. I crawl to the side, dazed, the Reese's wrapper still
stuck to my palm.

Later, completing the incident report in the office, I sit rolled
in a scratchy brown blanket, feeling like a human Ho Ho, staring at the end of my narrative. I'm supposed to sign it, and I
will. But I wish I knew if I knew the Reese's wrapper was there

all along. Tommy made his choice once he saw it, disappearing without even a splash, and I can live with that; he always liked to live life on his own terms; maybe his end was his valentine to himself. The thing I want to know is if I made my own choice. I mean, when I offered him my hand, what was I offering him?

I close my eyes and rest my forehead on the cool metal table, lips moving as if I'm talking, or maybe as if I'm praying. I'm not, it turns out. I'm saying a name.

When I realize that, I sit up and sign the paper, mountains and blue skies ahead of me, rivers and lakes, thrilled to be alive, thinking, *Maybe she'll know, maybe Donna can help me figure it out.*

Home for the Holidays

We were simmering Rueben on the front burner until the report cards came in, at which point I turned up the heat.

Pretty soon he was screaming to be let out, so I grabbed him with the tongs and dropped him in the colander to let him cool off. Study, I said, after we poured him on the paper towel. He made a big show of how his skin was shedding—like I was going to regret having left him in too long—but I didn't have time for it. Katie was boiling over on the back burner, since we hadn't stirred her in a while, and my wife was looking for the oven mitts.

They don't put anything back, I said, and glanced at Rueben again. He was still red—more than the other kids, he shows his cooking—but he didn't have anything to say to that. Just reached down and pulled a piece of overdone spaghetti from between his toes and held it up, as if to say, See, I told you.

Kids today. The littlest bit of heat and they start to melt.

Worst thing is when they boil on their own and the burners aren't even on. You run into the kitchen at the noise, grab the handle not knowing it's hot, and get a terrible burn; the scar lasts a lifetime. They tell you it fades away but it doesn't. If you hold your hand under the hood light there it is, two undiminished pink tracks across the creases of your palm. We've both got them on both hands, at least one from each kid, and I can tell you exactly where I got every one of them. Even on my deathbed I'll be able to; some things you just don't forget: sauces that split,

arguments over broccoli, the time we were convinced Emily
would make a great baked Alaska. That one I feel bad about,
but with kids, you don't have much time for regrets; too many
new things pop up. They climb in each other's pots, or yell if
you lift the lids, they turn into these weird nocturnal creatures
when they go through puberty and you stumble downstairs in
the morning to find that in the saucepan you left your daughter
in is this unfamiliar oval face, like a possum. Of course, it must
have been the same for our parents, and theirs, and theirs, all
the way back to the first humans and the invention of fire.

It's only at the holidays, when they're all contentedly bub-
bling away in a half-dozen pots and my wife's in the warming
drawer, her mother cooling in the fridge, that I'm happy. That's
the way it should be: everyone in one place talking about their
days and me watching over them, tempering the heat, adjusting
the spices (Emily takes a lot of salt), stirring the kids with an old
wooden spoon to keep them from burning (especially Rueben,
who's always had a tendency to stick to the bottom of whatever
pot he's in), dipping my face into the fragrant steam, savoring
what's to come.

Peace.

Three Hundred Words of Grief

Come home, her mother said. Her voice sounded small on the phone, her British accent oddly pronounced.

Gael pushed herself away from the counter with her hip. What? she asked, buying time. On the floor a conga line of red ants circled some spilled honey and she resisted the urge to squash them with her shoe. What did her mother mean by home? She hadn't lived with her for years. Not a place but a time then; home had been long ago.

I went to the doctor's today, her mother said. About some tests. On the way home, I saw a hearse.

Of all things, Gael said, trying to be as brave as her mother. She knew she couldn't talk long, her throat already clogging. She dampened a sponge and wiped away the honey. Her breathing was ragged even to her own ears, but her mother didn't pick up on it, though normally she would have. The old barn owl, she and her sisters used to call her.

Can you come up? her mother asked. For Easter? I know it's your favorite time to be with the kids, but could you?

Of course, Gael said, standing and feeling winded, lost in the apparition of childhood Easters: her mother's long fingers dipping warm eggs in dye, vermilion or marine-blue or pomegranate red, crystal and silver sparkling on the dining-room table, awaiting the raucous dinner, the bitter disappointment of snow, which meant Gael couldn't wear her new Easter shoes to Sunday service. She cleared her throat, tossed the blue sponge into the porcelain sink. Such a normal thing to do. Listen, she said, her voice a whisper; anything else would choke her. The kids are in the car, waiting. I have to go. I'll call back when I have my ticket.

She hung up, glad that she'd made it before her voice betrayed her. It wasn't a conversation to have on the phone.

Her sister Cait met her at the airport. Behind her thick new glasses her blue eyes looked huge.

How's Mummy? Gael said.

Not good.

I know. I guess I just hoped it would be all wrong.

No. It never is. She took Gael's bag and walked with it, letting it bump against her hip every other step. Gael resisted the urge to tell her it had rollers; Cait had always complained of Gael's bossiness.

And then look at those fatties, Cait said, nodding at a group of jumbos dressed in orange sweats and buying industrial-sized bags of caramel popcorn from a gaudy pushcart. They already had hotdogs and sodas and boxed candy. How come they're not sick? she said.

I don't know, Gael said, and smoothed her hair. Maybe they already are.

Sure, Cait said, and switched hands on the bag so that now it was between them. But they're not dying.

Under the covering blanket her mother looked no bigger than a Christmas turkey, her arms—where they showed—slim and bruised. They were cleaning her mother's mouth with a swab, Claudine trying to force her mouth open while Angelo held her head still.

Hi, Sweetie, Angelo said. Her father, always thin, had

passed beyond skeletal to spectral. It was almost as if he were the one dying. Under his translucent hands her mother made a gurgling noise.

Is that for us? Gael said, of the swabbing. Because her breath is bad? She wanted to stop it if it was; her mother was uncomfortable, gagged. Why couldn't they let her be?

No, Claudine said, for her. It keeps her from getting infections. Here, Mum, Claudine said. Open up.

She wouldn't.

I know you don't want to, but you have to. Let's just get through it. She pinched her mother's nose shut and Bernadette's mouth opened like a turtle's, thin and lipless. Claudine swabbed her gums and their mother's tongue came out and latched onto the long pink swab. Claudine had to tug to get it out and her mother's head jerked when she did. Gael turned away.

I'm going to put my things in a drawer, she said. Call me when you're done.

I'll help you, Angelo said, and walked beside her down the hall, one hand on her shoulder. She only noticed it after several steps, after which she reached up to pat it, the bones so prominent they felt like mountain ridges. Neither of them spoke.

For long stretches Gael sat by the bed, reading while her mother slept, sweating, her hands and face swollen. She'd moved the mirror from the bureau in case her mother was able to sit up. She wouldn't want to see herself, the big pie-face that many of her countrywomen had had but that she'd avoided her whole life.

Primary mediastinal B-cell lymphoma: This type accounts for about 2% of all lymphomas. The cells are large. This lymphoma starts in the mediastinum.

The clink of metal on metal roused her. Claudine stood at the edge of the hospital bed, one hand gripping the metal rail, checking their mother's pulse against the watch on the underside of her wrist. The blue X of veins beside her left eye was there, as always, and—as always—it surprised Gael. One vein started at the eyebrow and dipped toward her earlobe; the other began below the eye and crossed up toward the temple. The vivid blue paled her skin and made Claudine look young and vulnerable, an impression contradicted by the practiced way she let go of their mother's arm.

Gael said, How is it?

About the same.

Is that good?

It isn't bad.

Gael searched through the article for a word. What's the *mediastinum*? she said.

Media-*steye*-num, Claudine said, correcting her pronunciation. The area around the heart behind the chest bone.

Gael looked at the article again. And the superior vena cava?

The big vein that returns blood to the heart from the arms and head.

Gael wished again that she'd taken her mother's advice and gone to med school. At least then she could *do* something. She put the article down and picked up *The Liver Cookbook* from her mother's table. Green paper clips marked favorite recipes— Venetian liver and cranberries, deviled chicken livers, brandied chicken-liver mousse spread with thyme, brandy and yellow onions. A few of them looked delicious.

I should have known from her breathing and from that, Claudine said, her eyes watery. Mum never liked liver before. She must have thought she was anemic.

Their voices seemed to rouse their mother. I can't go east or west, or north or south, she said. Then she opened her eyes and looked at Gael. Are you sneaking in the salt and pepper?

When she closed them again she began to snore almost immediately and Gael remembered a trip from years before, when she'd surprised her mother.

Gael had come in unexpectedly and her mother said, Oh, hi, honey. Is that your baby? Her voice was friendly but flat. She'd thought Gael was perhaps one of the neighbor's kids. Then, recognizing her: It's Gael! And Deirdre! She'd glowed with delight, as if the sun had risen inside her. It was selfish and wrong to want that recognition again with her mother dying, Gael knew. Still.

How could it happen so fast? she said. She only called me Monday.

It happens at this age, Claudine said. Very fast.

Can it be slowed down?

Claudine tucked her mother's arm under the sheet without looking at Gael. It's a blessing, really, the way it happens. When it drags out it's even worse.

Blessing? Gael thought. Was her sister religious now? She let it go. But I didn't get to talk to her, she said.

She can hear you.

When she's awake. But even then, most times, she doesn't make sense. This morning she asked if I'd bleached all the daffodils.

Claudine laughed. She wanted to know when I was saying Mass. Then she shrugged. I'm sorry. If I'd paid closer attention, we all would have had more time.

In the other room, their father blew his nose, repeatedly, honk after honk.

Bernadette, their mother, her eyes still closed, raised one arm and said, The call of the noble goose.

Emily came in with Mab, her daughter, bringing with them the scent of the cold outside air.

Mab stopped just over the threshold and glanced around the room. You don't have any candy or Easter eggs out, she said.

I know, honey, Gael said, and squeezed her tiny shoulder through the marine-blue wool of her winter coat. Next year.

Is that Mum's? Emily said.

Gael turned her arm up and looked at the cuff. The green robe. How many years had her mother had it? Yes, she said. I was chilly.

Well, good to see you, Emily said, and hugged her. They stayed downstairs with Mab while Emily went up to sit with their mother. Mab, only seven, wasn't allowed to go.

You don't want to, Claudine said. Nana doesn't look good.

I know, Mab said. The way she played with the yellow ribbon in her dark hair made her look older. My dad said once she gets like this all we can do is wait for the phone call. You shouldn't get your hopes up, Aunt Gael. I don't think there will be a next year.

Cait and Claudine looked at one another.

That's your dad, Cait said. President of the Optimists Club.

What's that? Mab said, standing. She seemed to shake with excitement. Can I join?

Gael said, I think you already have.

Outside the weather was horrible. Wet brown leaves plastered against the side of the garage, a thin white covering over the humped, muddy earth. Fat snowflakes fell intermittently, interspersed with freezing rain that tapped against the windows. This was spring? Though if she looked closely, here and there dark crocuses were pushing their furled maroon-tipped buds through the darker mounded earth, and a single bird sang in the bare pin oak on the front lawn, the same few shrill notes over and over. *A thrush*, she thought, though she had no idea how she knew; one of the many things she'd forgotten her mother teaching her, perhaps, like bits of trees and houses and old books surfacing in rivers far from their sources. When Deirdre found them in herself years from now she wouldn't recognize their origins either, which made Gael even sadder.

So when her cell phone rang she was glad for the distraction, though she didn't feel like talking with her husband or children just then.

The tulip poplars popped yesterday, her husband said. Forsythia's come and gone.

She could tell he didn't know what to say; the weather was always his fall-back conversational topic, safe and neutral, nothing to cause any pain. And yet he'd called, sensing that his voice might steady her. It gladdened her, even as it made her unaccountably tired. She said, All this, in three days?

Three hot days. Almost ninety. On the forsythia, the green is already showing through the yellow. You know the allée of it, near the old Dumesnil place? The brick road? It's already come and gone.

Not up here, she said. Up here it's three months ago.

Her husband sighed. I'm sorry it isn't, he said.

She knew what he meant; she'd have more time with her mother. She didn't want to think about it, to drop into silence; she'd cry then. I'm not, she said. She'd thought they were moving to the same city three months ago; she was going to get a job with a different company and be closer to her mother after years of hoping to be, but it hadn't worked out.

It would have been worse, she said. To call with that good news and then to get Mum's news in return. And I almost did.

For a few seconds he was silent and she wondered if he'd hung up without saying good-bye, which would have been unlike him. Then he said, Thank God for small favors.

Yes, she said, and then repeated it, Yes, yes, as if trying to convince herself. She said, That's all He seems to be granting us now.

After he told her what was meant to be a funny story about his incompetence at helping the kids dye Easter eggs, she let him go. She stood holding the warm phone, watching Claudine through the kitchen window, remembering when Claudine had gone off to college. Everyone in the house had been sad though nobody would say so because you were supposed to be happy for her and they were, but even so her departure felt like a puzzling loss. Cait had stood in the hallway outside Claudine's room staring at the stripped bed and said what they all were thinking: I never thought it would change.

That was the worst of it, Gael supposed, girding herself to go inside once more. The relentless future was always coming and though you hoped and planned and dreamed of and for it, still somehow you foolishly thought you could stave it off, or at least the worst parts.

At night, Gael and Emily and Claudine were in the kitchen. Claudine was drinking milk from the carton. Gael didn't even bother saying anything. What would be the point? Behind the milk was the lamb, shrink-wrapped in bloody plastic like something inside a womb. She wanted to throw it out but it would stink by the morning. Sunday night then, before the trash came the next day.

Claudine put the milk back and grabbed a cantaloupe. She might rally, she said, rubbing it almost tenderly.

Gael and Emily looked at each other.

I saw that, Claudine said, and began passing the cantaloupe from hand to hand as if juggling it.

What? her sisters said, in unison.

The look. I know you think I'm nuts.

You *are* nuts, if you think that. You said two days ago it was going to happen quickly, that you knew the disease.

Yes, I do, and now I'm saying she might rally. Might. Not for long, but there's a chance. I've seen it. She dropped the cantaloupe on the shelf again and shut the fridge and stepped into the darkness of the dining room.

Emily opened the fridge, her face yellow in its yellow light, and Gael asked her for the cantaloupe. She sniffed the overripe vine-end and began rubbing its dimpled surface.

What are you doing? Emily asked.

It's my crystal ball, Gael said. I want it to tell me whether or not to buy stocks.

Emily laughed. Gael did too. Then, over Emily's shoulder, she saw Claudine observing from the dining room, eyes shining in the reflected kitchen light like an animal come to watch, until she blinked and turned away.

Gael sat by the bed again. After a day, she'd realized she was there as much to keep the others company as her mother, who often didn't know who she was, or where. The boys were coming in another day. She'd wanted to dye Easter eggs—the way her mother had when they were young, striping the eggs with thin lines of tape or dotting them with stick-on paper-hole-reinforcers—but when she suggested it her sisters burst out laughing.

To keep herself busy she leafed through a box of old pictures. About every third one had some writing on the back. *Gael, seven and a half years, and ?* She couldn't read the writing. Susan? Sarah? Sandy? She didn't recognize the other girl, not even a flicker. Then an old one. *Five years. 1914.* She thought she saw a family resemblance in the full curving upper lip of the women sitting three abreast in the back seat of an open touring car, dressed in feathered hats as if for church, but she might have been wrong. Still, they must have been family, mustn't they? Why else would her mother have saved the pictures? She wished she could find out and determined to bring the pictures home, even if she'd never know. Throwing them out seemed wrong. One more thing she should have asked when she had had the chance. She put the box down when her mother spoke.

Thar she blows!

What, Mum?

What, Mum? her mother said. Gael was surprised by how perfectly she'd mimicked her.

How did we have Christmas this year? her mother said.

We have Christmas every year, Mum.

Really?

Yes.

Ho ho ho. She shifted her hand from her hip to her chest and frowned. But I don't want to have Christmas this year. It makes my feet hurt.

We don't have to, then.

No Christmas?

No.

Then what will you do with the bunnies?

What would you like me to do with them?

What? She was agitated, frowning.

I'll feed them, Mum. The bunnies.

You will?

Yes.

Then what will you do for the kids for Easter?

I'll give them candy.

That's not funny.

It made her laugh to the point that she had to leave the room, worried she'd hurt her mother's feelings.

An hour later she opened her eyes and looked at Gael. I love you a bushel and a peck.

Was she conscious? Gael felt her throat closing. I love you too, she said. Her mother's eyes were shut; she might not have heard her. Who could tell? She got up to stretch her legs.

One, two, three, four.

Angelo, night-shirted, hovering white and ghostlike in the dim doorway, said, Mother, what are you doing?

I'm counting.

I know that. Why?

It helps me to sleep.

But Mother, he said, turning both palms up as if to show her something, that's the tenth time you've counted to twenty.

So let me get back to it. Otherwise, it won't work. And I'm not your mother. *One! Two! Three!*

It was exhausting even listening to it; he hadn't slept a full night in weeks. He rubbed one shiny hairless shin up and down on the other calf and turned away.

Gael was in the kitchen by herself, making food for her sisters and father. A few sandwiches that she wrapped up, avocado and turkey and Swiss cheese she'd trimmed the dry edges from, some pierogies that she boiled before frying, rice pudding sprinkled with cinnamon and nutmeg, the lone Portuguese recipe her father had taught her. In the spice drawer she had to search awhile to find the paprika, and its scent was dull, barely tickling her nose. Normally her mother's spices worked on Gael like snuff. She made a mental note to shop for spices, then thought better of it. Other than her mother, no one was likely to use them.

She decided to make a pie, something her mother would like, rhubarb and strawberries. Tart and sweet. Whenever she made crusts, she always heard her mother's voice, as she'd been a natural teacher. *Roll from the middle out, and change directions. You don't want to heat it up too much by overworking it, and the changed directions allows it to cool down.* She made piecrusts by feel, not by measurement; measurements could be thrown off by heat or cold, by dry weather or wet. Now as she worked, Gael had, as she often did, the sensation that it was her mother's hands doing the work and not her own. Tonight it was eerie, and she hummed to distract herself. The same few notes, which came from no song she remembered, so she switched to the lullabies her mother had sung to her in this very kitchen and which she in turn had sung here and elsewhere to her own children.

The aroma of baking pie filled the house—caramelized sugar and lemon zest and cinnamon; the rich, rounding crust. But it was late, so only Claudine came down to see what it was. The pie glistened on the counter as if Gael had glazed it.

Claudine crossed her arms under her large chest and said, Why'd you make that?

I like it, Gael said. She slipped off the old red-and-white striped oven mitt, automatically nesting it in the utensil drawer.

You'd better. No one else is going to eat it.

Why not?

Claudine shrugged. Too fattening.

I don't think a single slice will kill anyone.

But no one eats just one, Claudine said, and bent to sniff it with closed eyes, as if partaking in a sacrament.

I can, Gael said.

Prove it, Claudine said, and nudged it over the counter toward her. Gael took out a knife and cut the pie exactly in half. This one is mine, she said, tapping the closer half.

Claudine grabbed a fork and began eating the other half. Oh my God, she said. This is Mummy's crust. I wish I could make it too.

You could, Gael thought, *if only you'd paid attention.*

Her sisters had been merciless teasers about her time with her mother in the kitchen, none worse than Claudine, who'd given Gael the loathed nickname Mother May I. Now Gael thought, *Let it go. No reason to get out the backhoe and unearth everything.* With her thumb, she pushed aside a stray blond hair that had drifted over Claudine's eye. Too busy eating, Claudine seemed not to notice.

They ate like it was a pie-eating contest and they couldn't stop laughing, now and then cleaning a bit of crust or a dangling strawberry from the other's mouth or chin, racing to be

the first one done, though at the end Gael found it a bit discon-
certing. After finishing, Claudine pointed her stained fork at the
pie and said, We ate 110%!—their mother's least favorite cli-
ché—and laughed again. Her lips and tongue were stained red,
which looked to Gael too much like blood.

At six the next morning Gael woke to bright sunlight and noises
in the kitchen and found her mother sitting on a small chair in
front of the open refrigerator.

It made the hair on the back of her neck stand up. *A ghost*,
she thought—especially her mother's hands and feet, so white
they looked formed from freshly fallen snow. Then Bernadette
turned her head, revealing yellow eyes.

What day is it? she said, extending her arms from the green
robe. Her bruised wrists looked beaten.

Today? Gael glanced at the sunlight streaming through
the lace curtains, light so pure it seemed the days of rain had
cleansed the air. Sunday, she said.

The twentieth? Happy Easter.

Gael, remembering the Easter brioches her mother made
every year, the bread as yellow as pound cake yet as light as
cotton candy, debated lying, but her mother was likely to see
a paper and then she'd get angry. No, Mum, she said, resting
one hand on her mother's frail bony shoulder, which felt as if it
might crumble beneath her touch. Ashes to ashes, dust to dust,
it was already happening; it didn't matter how much either of
them wanted it not to. No, Mum, she said again, and squeezed,
the lightest pressure, a moth's wings beating the air. It's the
twenty-seventh.

I missed a week?

Slept right through it.

Greek Easter? she asked, and then shook her head. Gael
guessed she was sad to have missed any of her little time

remaining. That's okay, her mother said. Greek Easter. The weather's changed, she said. That's good. She pushed the chair aside with her yellowed ankle and shut the fridge and stood, holding the bloody lamb, wobbling under its weight. I can be Greek for a week. A little marjoram, some oregano, we'll be fine. And cucumber. You'll have to get that for the tzatziki. I think I have enough olive oil though. On that we should be okay. Maybe some mint.

In the sink the pie pan and the knife and two forks were soaking in dirty water. Gael wondered if Bernadette would say anything, or if she should, but Bernadette let the water out and slit open the package of lamb and the blood spilled out along with the rich, ruddy smell of meat. Crimson dots on the white counter.

Look at that, her mother said, dragging together an archipelago of spots with her fingertip, which she touched to her lips and tongue. Almost like we cut its throat ourselves.

They both reached to clean it up, two blue sponges. Their hands were bloody with the lamb's blood. She would be dead within a week, she knew, but it didn't matter. She was in the kitchen, cooking with her daughter, and the room was filled with light.

Acknowledgments

My thanks to the editors who first published these stories, and always improved them.

Thanks too to the incredible team at Sarabande Books: Sarah Gorham and Jeff Skinner for their initial interest in the book and inexhaustible ongoing support, Kirby Gann for his deft, insightful editing, Kristen Radtke for her acumen and energy, Kristen Miller, who shepherds the passage of so many good books into the world, and Emma Aprile for her precision.

Greatest thanks of all to Anne, whose love provides the light and space for all I write. Ne plus ultra.

The stories in this book originally appeared, in slightly different form, in the following publications: "Animati" in *Tin House*; "Newbie Was Here" in *Narrative*; "On Board the *SS Irresponsible*" in *Five Chapters* and *Sojourn*; "Immanent in the Last Sheaf" in *Vestal Review*; "The Caricaturist's Daughter" in *Juked*; "Separate Love" in *Velocity*; "Balloon Rides Ten Dollars" in *Juked*; "Open Season" in *One Story*; "The Wind, It Blows Forever" in *North American Review*, "Mum on the Rocks" in *North American Review*.

Paul Griner's first book, the story collection *Follow Me,* was a Barnes & Noble Discover Great New Writers pick. His next two books, the novels *Collectors* and *The German Woman,* have been published in half a dozen languages. His work has appeared in *Ploughshares, Playboy, One Story, Tin House, Narrative,* and *Zoetrope,* among others. He's a Professor at the University of Louisville. His novel *Second Life* was recently published by Counterpoint/Soft Skull.